Heart on for Dragon

A
Dragon Guard
Holiday
Love Story

Dragon Guard
Holiday Love Stories
Book 3

JOIN THE CLAN

Wanna keep up with all my crazy? Have fun? Win some cool prizes? Get *exclusive* excerpts to upcoming books?
Sign up for my newsletter RIGHT HERE!

Be the FIRST to see new covers, sneak peeks, and best of all, ADVANCED COPIES OF ALL MY BOOKS!!!
Join the group! Julia's Mills' Fan Club on Facebook!

I absolutely LOVE stalkers! Here's all the links! Follow me everywhere!
Newsletter
Website
Facebook
Instagram
Twitter
Pinterest
BookBub
Goodreads

ACKNOWLEDGMENTS

Edited by Em Edits
Proofread by Book Nook Nuts
Beta Read by Linda Levy, Ann Ivey,
and Beverley Pritchard

For my girls

HEART ON FOR DRAGON

**I've got a Heart on for my Dragon and nuthin' stops a
Brown Witch - not even you!**

Valentine's Day went off without a hitch. Love was in the air.
Arrows were flying. The chocolate-covered cherries were
extra good, and...
Drum roll please...
My hunka-hunka-burning love returned from parts
unknown.

Everything was wonderful. The world was in love. I was in
love. Even Bernie smiled for half-a-second
And then it happened...
Bibiddy-bobbity- blech-ack-gag-gag-gag!

Whisked across the galaxy, thrown into a hole in the ground
and separated from my Dragon, my happily ever after was
brutally rebuffed and Goddess help us all, somebody
touched my butt!
This crap will not stand!

Just let me get my Magic back and I'll be opening a can of
whoop ass and not even asking for initials or my name's not
Violet E. Brown, Witch Extraordinaire and Keeper of the
Spark of Love!

Watch out, bad guys! Back up Spiorpion! My spellin' fingers
are cocked and Bernie's fit to be tied! We're coming to save

my Dragon Man, jerk a knot in your tail, and send you back to the Hell from whence you came.

Valentine's Day may be over, but the Love only stops when I say so. That's my gig. That's who I am. Amoré is what I do! Ya' hear me, Bad Guy?

PART I

CAN I GET A LITTLE LIGHT ON THE SUBJECT?

"What the *hell* have *you* done?"

"What have *I* done? What the hell have *you* done? This is *your* world, I'm just an innocent bystander – a visitor, Sweetheart."

"Oh, my Great Goddess, don't even *think* about shoveling that load of Dragon crap my way, Michael Alexander Archer! Just don't do it. It's been a really bad day. I mean colossally bad and just 'cause..."

"It's Mick, dammit. My name is Mick, my beloved one and only Mate that I love with all my heart. Mick. Not Michael. Not Dick. Not Asshole. Mick. M-I-C-K. And *you* know it."

"I love you, too, but that does not..."

"Hang on, I'm not finished." The sound of a single boot heel scuffing the ground sounded from somewhere to my left as my dazzling Dragon continued to bitch. "It reminds me of my mom, and you know, better than even the Goddess herself, that I *never* want to think of *that* woman. Not ever again for as long as I live. She and Big Daddy are poison. Rotten to the core. They are..."

"Yes, Honey, I understand, but..."

"Please, Vi, I'm almost done," he huffed, his irritation taking the form of a loving Magical bop to the back of the head. "I mean, I love you. I have always loved you, and I always will. For the first moment I saw you, Violet Elizabeth Brown, you have been the beat of my heart, the light of my soul, the most gorgeous and amazing woman in the whole wide world that was made just for me, but I just cannot stand it when..."

"Okay, my turn," I cut in, letting *my* exasperated Magic lead the way. After all, turnabout *is* fair play and all's fair in love and war.

(FYI – this was love.)

"The fact that you came all the way to the Kingdom of Love sitting on the one and only Cloud Nine clear on the other side of the whole dadgum Realm to see me - to be with little old *me* after so many years was wonderful. I mean, seriously amazing and I love ya' for it more than I already did. But just 'cause I adore you more than all the chocolate covered cherries in the whole wide world and I can't see the nose on my face don't think for one minute that I *won't* zap your scaly ass from here to the shores of the Isle of Skye and back again. This is your mess. I'm just sure of it. Something you did or somebody you pissed off has taken their revenge and thrown us into... umm, I mean, tossed you, me, and Bernie into..."

"You know it wasn't me, Violet. I've not been back long enough to piss anybody off."

Ignoring his rebuttal, my arms flew in every direction as I spun around trying to see something – *anything* - in the pitch-black darkness, I was on a roll. There was just no stopping. There was a point to be made, and dammit, I was gonna make it. As my Granny used to say, *"Vi could have an argument in an empty elevator."*

(As I'm sure you can imagine, that used to piss me off. But after about a century or two, I got over it. It's not like I was ever going to zip my lips or the Old Lady, as we affectionately called her, was ever gonna hush. Now, that I'm older and a bit wiser, I consider my ability to talk my way out of any situation or blab until the other guy just gets tired and gives up – my Superpower.

Yes, I'm a Witch – a Brown Witch to be exact. One of the strongest of the strongest, the best of the best. But so are all my cousins, so in our Family Magic is like buttholes – everybody's got one. So, as you can imagine, I was forced to find my own special way to stand out. Long story short – or long story longer, as the case may be – Talking is my Superpower. Okay, enough of that. Back to the story...)

"Umm, well, crap, Mick, I don't know where we are, but that doesn't matter. I will goose that sexy ass of yours, Dragon Man. You know I will. As soon as I figure out where we are and who you smarted off to, it'll just take the tiniest twitch of my pinky fingers and you're gonna be hootin' and hollerin' just like that time..."

"You. Will. Not."

"Oh yes, I will. Just as soon as I can see where we are, I swear I'm gonna Magick us right back to my little white cottage with candy-apple red shutters and pretty pink roses growing in the flower boxes and we're gonna sit down and have one helluva long talk. And for the love of all the little hearts tattooed on all the little butts of all the little Cherubs in the whole damned world would you, *puhlease* get your big, ole, Dragon hand off my ass. It's not that I don't..."

"That's not my hand."

"...like when you touch me. *You*, of *all* people, *know* how *very* much I love when you touch me. But do you really think now is the time? And do I need to remind you what happens when you piss off a Brown Witch? Specifically, *this* Brown Witch. I swear to all the rosebuds on all the bushes all over Cloud Ni...WHAT?! What did you say? That's not your...?"

Jumping straight into the air as if I'd been shot out of a cannon, I started spinning around on my toes like some demented ballerina on a sugar high after rapidly ingesting one-hundred-and-fifty-three-thousand pixie sticks. But that wasn't enough. I could still feel whatever it was tickling my bodaciously awesome booty.

It was warm and huge, and Goddess help me, it was moving...

Hopping around like a Great Horned Toad on catnip, my arms flung hither and yon in directions no one's arms have ever flapped in the history of forever. I mean, I'm not even sure they were supposed to move like that – but they damned sure did.

(Thank the Goddess for Magic and the flexibility of being part of the Supernatural Community.)

Shrieking and screeching, I finally got my flying appendages under control, wrapped them around my wonderfully curvaceous physique, and began slapping *both* cheeks of my perfectly proportioned behind to the tune of Dueling Banjos like they were on fire.

(And, yes, for your edification, I was still screaming like my cousin, Birdie, the Banshee and talking faster than an auctioneer at the Rockefeller's estate sale.)

"Who is it? What is it? Who's touching me? *What's* touching me? Great Goddess in go-go boots, get it the hell off of me! Is it a spider? It better not be a spider, Mick. I hate those little sons of bitches. Oh shoot, oh shit, oh schnickeys, is it a scorpion? Please, please, please, tell me it's not a scorpion. I know they're poisonous. No! no! No-no-no-no-noooooo! What if it's a *spiorpion*?! They're ten times as poisonous as anything else anywhere in the whole damned world. I mean, we may not still be on Earth, but please tell me it's not a spiorpion. I read about those nasty little buggers in National Geographic. They are soooooooo poisonous and they hate Witches. I just know they hate Witches. The article didn't say they hate Witches, but I'm somehow sure my ancestors pissed off one of their ancestors - it's just what those old girls did - and now the eight-legged freaks with pinchers and antennae and a venomous stinger poking out of their butts – are out for blood. My blood! My blood, Mick! What if...?"

And that's when my wonderful, fantastic, sometimes might need a smack to the back of the head Mate responded with all the care and concern of a man wanting to calm his Witch down, keep his cool, always be the hero, and most of all, get his facts straight...

"A spiorpion? What in all that's holy is a spiorpion? Do they even exist? Did you just make that shit up? You did, didn't you? Yep! You did. I just know it."

Interjecting a huge inhale that was like a cross between a groan and a growl, he started again, his tone more like a big, burly, sexy man trying coax a kitten out of a tree than a big, burly, sexy man trying to calm his Mate.

"It's all gonna be ok, Violet. I promise it is. You're freaked out and you want me to be just as freaked out as you are. It's natural. You think it will make you feel better if we're both losing our minds, but it won't. Trust me, Babe. Lost in the plot is not a good look for me. I'm your man - *your Dragon*.

I've got this. I've got you. I don't need to be all crazy Dragon dude to save the day."

Another inhale - this one *without* the grumble and growl and through his nose by the sound of it, my man was working double time to save the day. Sadly, I was pretty much inconsolably freaked out and nothing short of Auntie Belinda's Knock-Out Spell was going to work, but...

I tried to chill out. Really, I did. I hung on every word of Mick's little speech. Focused on every syllable, the calm, steady beat of his heart, the love in his voice. I even took deep breaths.

But instead of calming down, I got light-headed, inhaled dust bunnies the size of Bugs Bunny, and damned near choked on a pebble. Short of passing out, I feared there was no hope – however, my man kept right on being the best dadgum Mate the Universe ever created.

"Remember to exhale, Vi. Deep breaths are good, but you gotta let it out sometime. Here, do it with me."

I appreciated the effort. Really, I did. Loved him all the more for it. I knew in my heart of hearts that Mick would always have my back. He was the cherry on my sundae, the wind beneath my broomstick, *blah, blah blah*. That and all the other mushy sentiments I couldn't think of at the moment. Mick Archer was one of the good guys and he was all mine.

However, none of that did one blasted thing to negate the fact that something creepy was *still* touching my ass. No matter what I did, the little buggers refused to go away.

Not one to ever give up, still inhaling and exhaling, speaking to me in his deep, creamy baritone, the sounds of the scuffing of the heels of his boots filled the inky, creepy darkness as I continued to jump, skip, hop, twirl, cuss and squeal. Mick was trying to find me. Knew from experience that his touch would settle my frayed nerves better than anything else ever could.

(Again, I have to say – my man is the best ever. Even when he can't give up the fight...)

"By the way, I still can't quite believe that National Geographic had an article about something as asinine and unbelievable as a spiorpion. I'm just sayin', we're gonna look that shit up as soon as we get out of here, 'kay? Now, stand still and chill out, Baby. Hold still. I'm gonna...*oooooh! Ow! Shit! Ouch! Son of a blacked-eyed Badger! Ow! Ow! OWWWWWWWW!*"

(It is important for you to know that I neither stood still nor chilled out. I couldn't. That ship had sailed, and Mick should've known that. I was on Crazy Violet Island and that was all there was to it. Until...)

At the alarming sounds of awful distress coming from my hunka-hunka-burning love, my Mate, my Dragon, the only dude I'd ever loved and would ever love, the someday-daddy of my babies, the man the Universe made just for me - all motion stopped.

(Lookie there. Who woulda thought it? That was all it took for me to chill the hell out and get my head on straight. Bring my ass back from Crazy Violet Island. Shame we didn't think of it sooner.)

With my hands out to the side like I was about to take off, my booty stuck out as far as it would go, and my eyes open so wide it felt like they were about to take over the entire surface of my cute-if-I-do-say-so-myself face, I apologetically squeaked, "Oh, my Goddess, Mick. I am so sorry! Are you okay?"

"No worries, Sweetie," he ground out through what I didn't have to see him to know were gritted teeth.

(The gnashing and grinding of enamel was a sure tip off.)

"I'm good. Just, umm, maybe next time, when you're… umm freakin' out over imaginary bugs and hopping around like you've got ants in your pants, maybe you could jump away from me, and not on my toe."

"Oh, no," I cooed, honestly upset that I'd stomped on my honey's tootsies and really, really regretting that I'd gotten freaked out thus causing what will go down in the annals of Brown-Archer history as the Jumping on the Foot incident.

(I told Mick not to share that story with his brothers and my cousins. But did he listen? No, no, he did not.)

Inching the toe of my cherry red Chuck Taylors across what I prayed was a floor and not the burial ground of a herd or a horde or *legion* of whatever had been on my behind, I tried with all my might not to once again freak out and inadvertently step on my sexy Dragon. "Are you okay? Stay right where you are. Let me get over there and I can fix ya' right up. I'll use Dr. Bombay's Heal Anything Any Time Anywhere Spell. He said I was the fastest learner he'd ever seen and most proficient of all. Heck, he wants me to take some of his house calls once we're all settled in back on Earth. Just give me a sec, and I'll have you fixed right up."

"I'm not sure you should…"

"Oh, stop," I pshawed, pushing my arms out in front of me and flicking my finger in the direction of the sound of Mick's voice. "I know you think that Dr. Bombay, who is in my humble opinion…"

"I love you, but you are *anything* but humble, *Mo chroí*."

"…the best doctor in the known universe and some we have yet to discover, should limit his practice to Witches."

"You betcha."

"I know. I know. I know, you think he's not had enough

practice with Shifters of any kind, specifically Dragons, to be treating..."

"I'll be damned," Mick chuckled.

(You have to admit, my man is lovable. Yes, I agree, he's irritating and sarcastic, but loveable and adorable top the list.)

His snickering growing to full blown, laughter, I swear he slapped his leg as he chortled, "You were listening. My Mate, the one and only Violet Brown, actually heard something I said. Mark this day on the calendar."

(Okay, so he had a point. Like I said before, I do tend to talk first and survey the situation later – but again, I reiterate – It. Is My. Superpower. So, you won't be surprised to hear that at this point it was a battle of wills and I refused to give in. That man, my man, *would* listen to me. I would honey and sweetie and pour on so much sugar Mick got a cavity in one of those big ole fangs of his Dragon's, and he *would* hear me. I would heal him with Doc Bombay's Spell and that was all there was to it. I am Witch. Hear me roar.)

"Un-huh, whatever. Like I was saying, you think that Esau, the Dragon King with whom you share your soul, a real powerhouse and spectacularly awesome Winged Warrior in his own right who I adore so very much and would be lost without aside from you of course, can handle anything and everything, but that's just not so."

"Yes, it is."

"No, *honey*," I stressed, trying really hard not to turn back into the crazy, nutball Witch from just a few seconds before because then Mick would completely stop listening and everything I'd said up to that point would have been for naught. "Dr. Bernardo Beltane Bombay, MD, Ph.D., PsyD, D.O., D.C and a whole host of other acronyms that we just don't have time for me to list but I will be sure to remind you of when we're safe at home, is certified for the treatment of any and all creatures great and small, winged and not-winged, human-looking and not human-looking, Magical and powerful, upside-down and ..."

"Violet," my man grumbled, his voice so low that it made my inner Witch bat her eyes and purr while my body got all hot and tingly and I almost – *almost* – lost my train of thought.

(By now you know me pretty well. So, you won't be surprised to hear that I was determined to make my point. Not even my libido was going to distract me. Yeah, I can be a real dipshit sometimes, but I am who I am.)

"Can you just..."

"Hang on, Hun," I nodded and held up the index finger of my right hand even though I was pretty sure he couldn't see it. "I'm almost done. I just need to make this point..."

"Yes, Violet, my love, I am *well aware* that you need to make your point. It is just one of the many, many things I love about you," Mick continued to growl. "But, right now, you have to..."

"...finish what I was saying. You are so right. Thank you, Honey. That's just the sweetest thing. Anyway, the Doc can fix anything, and he gave me this spell for just such an occasion because my job – my Calling, as it were – is to hang out on Cloud Nine in the Valentine Nebula on the other side of Everything in the Kingdom of Love and be the Magic that keeps Cupid in business. It's a really long trip, too long for the Doc to make except for the most serious of emergencies - even with his loads and loads of immense and powerful Magic. Isn't it wonderful that the most amazing Doctor in the history of Magical Mystical Medicine made sure I could take care of myself, as well as all the other Supes of Love in the Happiest Place in the Galaxy?"

"Yes, Sweetheart," Mick huffed, his voice at least an octave lower than usual and the scent of burning mesquite tickling my nose.

(Yep, you guessed it. That was a sure sign he was getting really close to goin' all scaly. Usually, it was a serious turn-on for me. I love the bright glittering bronze of Esau's scales, the Power and Magic that just rolls off of them both, and the way his voice rumbles in the deepest of baritones. However, on this occasion, I was too preoccupied to care. Again, I must say, I can be a real dipshit sometimes.)

"I know exactly where you've been and how long you've been there. And I am well aware of how far away it is. I am, after all, the one who came..."

I tried to zip my lips and listen. Really, I did. I mean, it was the least I owed my hunka-hunka-burning love after he'd defied Fate and Aphrodite's wishes to come to Cloud Nine to see me. It was the best surprise of my whole damned life, especially since I thought he was dead, or gone, or dead and gone. More on that in just a bit.

Best of all, my Mick helped me to prepare and pull off the greatest day of the whole danged year – the one and only Valentine's Day - and we got to celebrate said holiday in our own very special, *very personal* way. Oh, and just to be clear, it had nothing to do with Mick's grumbling that sounded more like growling with every passing second or the wonderful aroma filling my senses telling me Esau was about to make an abrupt appearance that had me reminiscing about being *with* my Dragon.

(Like, I said, I love me some Esau. He is the best. But...)

Seriously, I *wanted* to listen. Mick was my one true Fated Mate. He was the rice to my crispy, the bee to my hive, and the red sparkles on my jumbo box of chocolates. He made my heart go pitter-pat, my brain turn to mush, and visions of happily ever after dance merrily in my brain.

I *needed* to pay attention. I *knew* I did. There was something in the tone of his voice, or grumble, or growl - depending on what side of the conversation you stood – that made the Witch in the back of my brain scream, *"SHUT UP, VI! Something wicked this way comes! Turn off your mouth and switch on those innate and renowned problem-solving skills. Make with the hocus pocus. You're a Brown Witch for Goddess' sake! Get the lights on and Magick our happy heinies back the way we came. Witch, please! Get your shit together and get it done before we become Spiorpion Chow. HURRY UP!"*

Unfortunately, my mouth was on a roll that overrode my brain. My Superpower was working overtime to cover for the fact that I couldn't figure out what had been touching my butt and that in and of itself made not one damned bit of sense. 'Cause, if I'm honest, which I always am, and sometimes that's not such a good thing but it is what it is, I was *ob-sess-ing* over what I could have *possibly* mistaken for Mick's hand.

It just made no sense. My Mate was a *big guy* with *big hands*. I mean six-foot-six, broad shoulders, beautifully muscled chest, nice ass – *everything* on him was miraculously perfect and extra large in the best possible way. Michael Alexander Archer, aka Mick, as you might remember from just a few minutes ago, was sex on a stick and he was all mine.

Including the hand that *wasn't* touching my butt…

Looking into his beautiful brown eyes after so many years had been a dream come true. Running my fingers through his dark curly hair was nothing short of Heaven. Having his hands all over me was utter bliss and that's coming from the Brown Witch who is the one and only

Keeper of the Spark of Love, Second-In-Command of Cloud Nine, and Cupid's Right-Hand Witch with a capital W. If anyone knew bliss – it was me. It was my *Thing*. I zapped the golden arrows with *Amore* for the God of Love and his army of Cherubs to spread tenderness, adoration, and good old-fashioned L-O-V-E all over the world on the best day of the whole damned year – Valentine's Day.

Being with my Dragon was all I'd ever wanted for as long as I could remember, but none of that helped with the fact that something really big and warm and 'hand-like' had been on my ass. It freaked me out in ways a Brown Witch – specifically me - should never ever never get freaked out. It made goosebumps dance the hokey pokey up and down my arms and the little hairs on the nape of my neck stand at attention as if *Reveille* was playing. It was disconcerting in the worst of ways, and I didn't like it – not one little bit.

So...

I just kept talking. Saying way more words than absolutely necessary at a speed rivaling something just short of breaking the sound barrier.

"And while we're on the subject, it's important to remember that calling Dr. Bombay a Witch Doctor – something you have done on numerous occasions - is a very sore subject. The slightest mention of that rather derogatory moniker dredges up very bad memories for good old Bernie. I think I told you. Didn't I tell you? Maybe it was Molly, or Ella, or... Oh, hell, here, just let me tell you again really quickly to be sure all our I's are dotted and our T's crossed."

"You told me. Molly told me. Ella told me. *Everybody* told me. Please, Vi, you need to..."

And still my lips flapped...

"Poor, poor Dr. Bombay spent a very cruel summer on an unnamed island somewhere on the other side of the world hanging from his thumbs, with his toes dangling over an active volcano, while naked native women with rather perky breasts fed him mangoes until the yummy yellow fruit pretty much ran right out of his ears. I've never had the nerve to ask him what a detail like 'perky breasts' has to do with the story or how much mango you have to eat before it comes out your ears, but I suggest you don't inquire either, Mick, honey. You've already..."

"Vi?"

"...upset Dr. Bombay on more than one occasion. Molly said that..."

"Violet? There's..."

"...you and Chris were making fun of the special Pregnancy Cookies and Pre-Natal Floral Tea the Doc formulated especially for her and the baby. Why would you do..."

"Violet. You need to..."

And as I continued to ramble and talk right over my Dragon, the voice of the little Witch in the back of my mind gave up the fight. She literally huffed in utter defeat, *"Oh, Vi, you have lost your ever-lovin' mind. I'm going into hibernation. Wake me if we survive."*

To which I gasped, *"Why I never."*

And that's when Bernie got involved.

(And who might Bernie be? Well, buckle up, Buttercup, and keep your arms and legs inside the vehicle. I'm 'bout to rock your world.)

Bernie – aka Bernice the Beautiful, Bountiful, and Beloved - is...

(Yes, you are so right. Cherubs have the stupidest given names. But once again, I digress...)

...the sassiest, snarkiest, and oh-so full of crapiest Familiar in the whole wide world. She is a Cherub who can only *be a Cherub* when she's on Cloud Nine in the Kingdom of Love on the Valentine Nebula because she pissed Cupid off with a horrible, terrible practical joke about three centuries ago.

I mean, come on, I have no clue what she was thinking. Who replaces the Arrows of Love with stale candy canes, puts a metric ton of black licorice candy in the chocolate covered cherry machine, and dumps a whole bottle of Magically enhanced ebony hair dye in the God of Love's amore-scented shampoo and conditioner on Valentine's Eve? Not even I'm that daring (or stupid) – and that's sayin' something.

As you can imagine, Cupid was pissed with a capital P-I-S-S-E-D. Dashing out of Hearts on Fire Castle in nothing but a bright red towel, our illustrious leader trampled all over the lavender and pink lawns of the Kingdom of Love, kicked open the door of Bernie's cute little blush-toned cottage, and cursed her heart-shaped booty right there on the spot. Apparently, fiery red sparkles, flaming hearts, and putrid Pepto Bismal smoke flew from his fingertips as he roared, "No more a Cherub anywhere but home. A Potbellied Pig you will be wherever you roam. No more arrows of love, no more Amore to share. You have gone too far, Bernice, on this I swear. Pink as the posies with a tutu as red as rosies, get from my sight before I turn you into a Sprite!"

And so, it was. My Familiar, the only Familiar to every Witch Brown entrusted with the Spark of Love since the beginning of the Brown Witches, Bernice was an adorable Cherub with rosy cheeks and perfect blond curls *as long as* she stayed in the Kingdom of Love, but as soon as she so much as stuck a toe over the edge of Cloud Nine – she instantly became a very pink Potbellied Pig with a permanent tutu and itty-bitty wings.

(Just to be clear, I had no say over the name of our

Kingdom either. Good Goddess, I'm not *that* old. You have to talk to the big guy and well, he's rather indis.. that is to say, he's... Oh, hell, just pay attention...)

"Ha! You never?" Bernie goaded, the raspy tone of her deep, sounded-like-she'd-smoked-one-too-many-cigars-but-truly-never-had voice tap dancing on every one of my fraying nerves. "That's rich. You have and you know you have more times than either one of us cares to remember. You, Violet Brown, have done anything and everything..."

"Shut up, Bernie," I fumed.

"Oh, I'll shut up," she exploded. "Just as soon as you pay attention to that overgrown gecko of yours. He's been tryin'..."

"Hey!" Mick adamantly objected. "That's just..."

But Bernie was on a roll and she was having none of it.

"...to get your attention for the last ten minutes. Hush it up, Violet. *Damn*, just zip those lips of yours, and stop freaking out over some creepy crawly taking a trip across your gluteus maximus. Hell, you used to play with worms, talk to the spiders in the barn like they were Charlotte, and save ants from that creepy little kid with spectacles bigger than his face and a box of magnifying glasses bigger than Uncle George's steamer trunk. Pull your head outta your ass and use at least one ounce of the good sense the Great Goddess gave you. For cripes' sake, get your shit together! Make with the Magic. Get some light on the subject. Do what you do, Witchy Poo. Some of us are dyin' over here."

(For future reference, I (A) Have a metric shit ton of good sense. I am *known* for my good sense and quick thinking. Ask anybody – but Bernie. Everybody I know will confirm this fact. They will say, 'Violet is the Queen of rational thinking and problem solving. We go to her for help all the time.' I have references if you need them. (B) I am not usually such a wuss when it comes to insects, arachnids, and the like – as explained by the Potbellied Pig aka Cherub aka my Familiar aka the giant pain in my ass, Bernice. I'm a Witch for Goddess' sake. Squeamish is not in the job description and spiders are part of the gig. And (C) I am not afraid of the dark. I know you hadn't said that yet, and surprisingly neither had Bernie, but I need to head that shit off at the pass. Ya' feel me? Okay, cool. Now, back to the story...)

Not wanting to admit out loud that Bernie's 'unpep talk' had actually cleared my muddled brain almost as well as my Dragon's screams of agony, I took her advice and called out, "Mick? Mick, honey, what were you saying?"

But this time, there was no answer.

I knew he was there. I could feel the warmth of his body and the extra heat supplied by none other than Esau – the Dragon King Extraordinaire. The scent of mesquite and true love and spicy chili peppers was all around me. Mick was there – no doubt about it.

So, why wasn't he talking? Heck, I couldn't get him to shut up and listen just a few minutes earlier. Wouldn't you just know when I wanted him to talk, the infuriatingly wonderful man had fallen silent.

Hands out in front of me, feeling around in the dark like all those stupid people in scary movies while hoping that I looked infinitely better than all those silly actors in the plethora of horror films I'd watched over the years, I tried with all my might to find the love of my life. "Can't you see in the dark, Mick, Honey? Isn't that one of the things Dragons can do? I mean, Witches can, too. But for some reason, my Magic isn't working. It's like somebody flipped a switch..."

"Like the lights are on but nobody's home?" Bernie snorted. "Nuthin' new there."

"Shut up, Bernice," I ground out through gritted teeth, using her given name to add extra oomph before cooing...

(Yes, I cooed. I admit, it was not my finest hour, but we'd been hurdled through space and time...

Okay, hang on, let me clarify. At that point in this adventure, I had absolutely no idea *what* had happened or where we were. Remember the beginning? Yeah, that. All I knew for sure was that I was in the dark – both literally and figuratively. Nothing new there, but I digress. The facts were – Mick, Bernie, and I were in my house planning our trip home when out of nowhere *a zap, a zing, a bang, and a boom* burst through the walls. In the blink of an eye, everything went dark then my skin felt like a million or so angry fire ants were chowing down like it was Thanksgiving and I was the turkey. However, I *am* one smart cookie – if I do say so myself – and having been tossed around the universe, ridden on more than one Bucking Broomstick Bronco, exactly two moonbeams, and the tentacle of a space Octopus on a dare, I could, with some authority, say that we were no longer on Earth and in fact being hurtled through Time and Space.

Okay, now you're up to speed...)

I needed to find Mick. I had to know *why* he wasn't talking. I mean, cute banter was our thing. Neither one of us knew when to hush up and listen. It was just what we did. I was made for Mick and well, umm, Mick was made for me.

I got as far as, "Mick, are you..."

When a mighty inhale damned near sucked every last molecule of O2 from the atmosphere before the whole place – a gross, dusty, cobweb-covered cave- was lit up like Times Square on New Year's Eve with the most gorgeous red, yellow, and orange Dragon Fire. And there he was, the man of my dreams, my hunka-hunka-burning love, not ten feet away, looking at me with love in his eyes and a frown on his lips.

Hey! Wait! A frown?

(Yeah, I know. I thought the same thing.)

Hands still in front of me, butt poking out behind me in my perfect imitation of a big red hen, and eyes – yep, you guessed it – still open really wide, I inhaled deeply and opened my mouth. I was just about to say something really, really, unimaginably stupid like, *"Well, shit, Mick, you had your Magic the whole time? Couldn't you have made with the flames from the very beginning? What took you so long? And, what the hell? Why are you frowning?"* When Bernie snapped to attention, stood on her hind legs and threw both hooves straight out in front and roared, "Holy Cherub in a dirty diaper, is that Cupid?"

And that's when all hell broke loose.

PART II

THE NERVE OF SOME PEOPLE'S KIDS

I really had no idea what was happening or how we got there. All I knew for sure, was that Vi and I were finishing up our plans to head to Nowhere, USA – our hometown and the place we wanted to settle down, build a house of our own, and raise our family. Six weeks in the Kingdom of Love was nice. Check...make that *Heavenly.* Time alone with my Mate was nothing short of the B-E-S-T, but we wanted to live where we first met and fell in love and where our people were. Family was everything to both of us and the best way to start our lives together was by being there for the birth of our niece – the first Brown/Archer child, a Dragon/Witch Combo I was praying was born with my sister-in-law's looks and my brother, Nate's, tenacity.

Of course, Bernie was incessantly bitching about the lack of suitcase space she was allowed, and I was ignoring the fact that no matter what she packed all she would ever be able to wear was that blasted red, frilly tutu. So, why was she complaining? Who knows or cares? As I explained to her, there is only so much room on the back of my Dragon and my Mate's bags came first.

One minute Vi was showing me the tiniest pair of pink socks, I'd ever seen, and the next, black, evil sorcery exploded in her kitchen like a stink bomb in the girls' locker room.

Okay, let me clarify...

I admit, to those of you outside the Other Community that *might've* sounded a little crazy. You probably said to yourself, *'This dude's one scale shy of a whole Dragon and couldn't fly with both wings and a good tailwind,'* but nothing could be farther from the truth. I do indeed have all my scales, and an expert flyer, and although I share my soul with an ancient Dragon King– I am in full control of all my faculties. Really, you can ask anybody.

So, let's rewind and I'll try to make everything at least as clear as mud...

I was *well aware* of how I got to the Valentine Nebula, onto Cloud Nine, and into the Kingdom of Love. Very aware and very happy to be there. Missing my Mate, the one and only, amazing and gorgeous Violet Brown had been my constant pastime for damned near as many years as I'd been alive. It started a really long time ago and was a long and winding road...

(Yes, I LOVE me some Beatles.)

...with more bumps than a Horned Toad's back, but Fate and Destiny finally got their shit together and after way too many years apart, I was reunited with the one woman in all the world made just for me. Chalk one up for the good guys.

You see, my name's, Mick Archer, or to some - mostly my mother who I don't talk about without losing my mind and my religion - or to because she is evil with a capital E right along with my good for nothing father...

(Now, don't go gettin' all judgmental. I have my reasons and I'm gettin' to them.)

...well, let's just not go there again. You already had a front row seat to my disgust at being called by my Christian name. If you've made it this far, you know all the details, and we'll leave it at that.

Suffice it to say, the only person in the world who can get away with using my given name – and even then, I can't help but bitch about it - is Violet. Just hearing my full name makes me think of my parents and let's just say, I do not *ever* want to think of *those people*. Not only are they the worst of the worst the world has to offer but topping the list of their dastardly deeds is plotting the death of my oldest brother's Mate so they could steal her Magic.

I wish I could say that was all they'd ever done to secure their place in Hell, but I can't. Let me see if I can explain this without taking up too much of your time. It's a really long story that goes back *a lot of years*, but you need some of the info to understand what comes next. So, I promise to keep it as short as possible. Think Reader's Digest version, cool?

Okay, here we go...

In the Other community, there are times that families with illustrious and long Supernatural lineages end up with no Magic at all. We call them Nulls. For the longest time, all of us Paranormals thought it was a genetic abnormality. Like, Mother Nature's way of thinning the herd without doing anything too drastic. I, Mick Archer, am here to tell you that it is most definitely, without a doubt, *a Curse*.

Stop shaking your head and calling me an idiot. Curses exist. It's a fact of life, of nature, of *everything*. Trust me. I know what I'm talking about because for the first couple of decades of my life, I had *no Magic at all*. All of us Archer boys – that's what the citizens of Nowhere, USA, and the

Other Community called us (Some still do.) – thought we, right along with our parents, were Nulls and that's all we'd ever be.

Thankfully, we were wrong. Sadly, the reason we went without Magic for so very long rested squarely on the shoulders of my parents.

The fact of the matter was, the Powers That Be - aka the Great Goddess, the Universe, Mother Nature, Fate, and her sister, Destiny – along with my Grandad and our Clan all knew that my mother and father – Big Daddy and Mother Archer as they liked to be called - were rotten to the very core. I don't mean litter bugs or take-a-penny-when-they-don't-really-need-a-penny or take the little bottles of shampoo from hotels *bad*. I mean *horrible* with a capital B-A-D, real assholes, false-faced pretenders, just true wastes of space who wanted nothing more than to steal Magic and harm Others whenever and wherever they could.

See, Big Daddy and Mother Archer went above and beyond to act like they were pillars of the community, put on a pretty face for everybody, and get in good with *anybody* Magical they ever met. My parents sat on every single committee, club, and women's auxiliary in and around Nowhere, USA. Even if there was something as silly as a boiled peanut eating contest with someone from the Other Community in attendance – they were there. They went to all the functions, shook all the right hands, kissed all the right asses, even donated to the Other Orphans Home, and spearheaded the Food Drive for the Displaced Shifters' Sanctuary every fall.

They were so well regarded that although not Magical, the Brown Witches invited them to Samhain Dinner without fail – which is really saying something. And that's not all. Cupid made sure a small squadron of his best

Cherubs delivered candies and flowers and even one of those fancy cookie bouquets every Valentine's Day. Hell, the Easter Bunny had them over to color eggs, and the list goes on and on. Big Daddy and Mother Archer were a *big deal in the Other Community.*

But there was one thing they didn't have, couldn't buy, and damned sure weren't able to schmooze their way into getting... Yep, you guessed it - Magic.

Like I said before, the Powers That Be knew mom and dad stunk worse than a bag of shit baking in the sun for a month of Sundays but couldn't do anything to stop their dastardly plans. They had to let everything play out just as it was written in the Book of Life.

You see, these powerful and omnipotent Beings hoped against all hope that my parents would deny the evil festering in their souls and try to be good people. It was one of their greatest wishes. So, when that didn't happen, all the Powers That Be could do was wait and see if my brothers and I were fruit from the rotten tree or good apples.

(FYI- we're good apples. Just wanted to be sure you got that.)

In one of the many tomes of knowledge passed down from the Ancient Dragons, Liam, brother number two – only eighteen months older than me and eleven months younger than Nate- and Mate to Vi's cousin, Ella, shared a very important passage with me. He said, *every soul – Other or Human - is born with some light and some dark. What the person chooses to embrace – the good or the bad – is what makes them who they are.*

Thank the Heavens, Nate, Liam, Chris and I innately chose the Light. It's just who we were – *and are.* Without that, we would've been lost - just like mom and dad – and wouldn't have been able to be with our one True Fated Mates.

And here's where the story takes an upward turn...

When the time was right and our parents had gone off to another of their charity functions, Grandad Archer showed up out of the blue and knocked on the door like it hadn't been twenty years since we'd laid eyes on him. Not even coming in for coffee – heck, barely saying, 'Hi', Old Man Dragon, as he's known by all, told all four of us that it was time to go. Funny thing is, we just went. No questions asked. We packed a rucksack, walked out the door, and never looked back. All of us just knew it was the right thing to do.

Out of the Swamp of Nowhere, USA, we flew all night on the back of Granddad's golden Dragon to the Isle of Skye, Scotland. There we met our Clan – our true Family - learned who we really were and trained to be Guardsmen.

As shocked as we were, there was no denying how right it felt. It was as if we were reborn on that day. Like everything finally made sense – especially the way each of us felt for our own very special Brown Witch.

(That part wasn't easy. Oh, hell, no, like I said, I missed Violet every minute of every hour of every day. It was hard as hell to be away from her and to know she thought I might be dead. However, it was necessary, and now, I will spend my whole life making it up to her. Okay, I got off track again. Back to the story...)

And we weren't the only ones. Some of our cousins had been through the same thing – born without Magic, felt the call of a Mate they couldn't claim, and had no clue they were blessed by the Universe until that all-important knock at the door. No, they didn't all have shitty parents, like my brothers and me, but not a one of them had it easy.

Anyway...

Being with our Clan, with Grandad, and finding out who we really were was the best thing that ever happened to all of us, second only to knowing that someday I would be able to claim Violet as my own. To be called upon to be the Universe's Winged Warriors, to be part of the honorable, loyal, and fearsome Dragon Guard was nothing short of miraculous. It was a true honor to find out that we, and all our kin, were part of the greatest Brotherhood in Supernatural history - tasked with protecting not only all Others but humankind and the Earth itself.

Well, not mom and dad, but you already guessed that. My parents couldn't be trusted to take out the trash, and unfortunately proved to be even worse than we thought as time ticked on.

I know, I shouldn't say what I'm about to say about the two people who made my life possible, but I call 'em like I see 'em and so will you as soon as you have all the facts. Those stupid assholes, aka Big Daddy and Mother Archer, literally had some grand plan to steal Molly's Magic – that's Nate's Mate and a Brown Witch to boot - along with all the Enchantment in the whole Brown Family Coven (The strongest and most revered Witches in the entire world and beyond.) and to extract the secret of the Sacred Pumpkin Molly protects by using the blackest of sorcery. They actually thought they could escape reprisal from the Powers That Be and the Authority of Others by hiding behind evil Magic and parlor tricks.

Those idiots - my parents only because I had no choice - had gris-gris bags and spells and talisman, chicken bones, and the corpse of a Raven for the Goddess' sake and who knows what else. Who cares?

The point is, they were willing to sacrifice Molly to get what they wanted - and let me tell you, even thinking about harming a Brown Witch is one of the *deadliest* sins an Other can commit. That Family – those very special Enchantresses - were all blessed by the Universe and the Great Goddess long before they were a gleam in their daddies' eyes. Each has a special destiny that keeps the world turning and all its inhabitants happy, healthy, and none the wiser to the evil that lurks in the shadows.

Best of all, this generation – my and Vi's – is when the Brown Witches are Mated to the Archer Dragons. Talk about good luck. Hell, I'm livin' in high cotton, my friends. Violet always has been and always will be the only woman for me. She is the light to my darkness, the beat of my heart, the other half of my soul, and my reason for living, and that, you can take to the bank.

(Sorry, about that. Just the mention of my Mate and my mind gets me all muddled. Now, where was I? Oh, yeah...)

In the end, Nate led the charge and we got there in time. Molly was saved. Mom and dad went to one of the deepest Pits of Hell to be Satan's Kitty Box Cleaners for the rest of forever and the Authority of Others got to put a big red X through the pictures of Big Daddy and Mother Archer on their wall of Supernatural Most Wanted posters.

Best of all, I was given the green light to court, woo, and basically beg Violet to be mine forever and ever amen. Thank the Goddess, it didn't take much convincing – just a trip to the Valentine Nebula on the other side of the Galaxy – but my girl's worth that and so much more.

Now, you're caught up. And I hope you can see why I feel the way I do about anything that reminds me of my parents. Now, back to the important stuff...

Like I was sayin', I knew what day it was and that the blast of black Magic was how we'd been tossed into a cave – just not why or exactly where. And then there was the question running around my mind and flying out my mouth in response to Bernie's shrieking, jumping, and pointing.

"Are you sure that's Cupid? I don't think that's Cupid. That looks like..."

Reaching out to grab Violet as she raced towards the misshapen, swaddled in thick cobwebs, lumpy as a two-hundred-pound sack of potatoes, non-moving pile of 'something' wearing what 'might' have been the God of Love's crown, I scooped my Mate's running feet off the ground, held her close to my chest and ordered, "You cannot touch whatever *that* is until we know for sure what *it* is."

"It's *got* to be Cupid, Geckobutt," Bernie sassily snorted, her curly tail swishing back and forth in the opposite direction of her frilly red tutu as she strutted across the long narrow cave we'd been tossed into. Turning to the side and lifting her back left hoof parallel to her front left hoof leaving her standing on the tip of a single hoof, she added with a sneer, "That's his crown, isn't it, you Scaly Snothead?"

"It looks like it, but..."

"What do you think, Vi? Please tell me that all the blood has not rushed from your brain, too," the Pig demanded.

"Well, umm..." Violet hesitated, her big brown eyes sliding back and forth between Bernie and me as she tried to decide who to make the maddest.

Shrugging, the movement making her shoulder rub against my chest, caused Esau, the Dragon King with whom I shared my soul, to happily grumble, *I hope she never stops that. Damn, I love when that little Witch gets all up close and personal,* the woman I loved more than life itself finally made up her mind. "I'm sorry, Bernie, but Mick's right. I can't really tell. It's covered with... with... with..."

Throwing her hand in the air and flitting her fingers towards what very well could've been the God of Love in mummified form, but something was telling me was most *assuredly not*, she added, "...that *stuff*. Yeah, It's the right shape, but I just... Ummm, well, I just can't tell for sure." Pulling her shoulders as close to her cute little ears as she could, my little Witch eeked out, "Other than that, I just don't know, Berns. Sorry."

"You don't know?" Bernie railed, all three hooves that were still in the air waving around like she was auditioning for Air Traffic Control at DFW. "How the hell do you work for a guy for hundreds of years and not know what his crown looks like? Have you not been paying attention? Did whizzing through Time and Space scatter your brains more than they were already wrecked? Do I need to come over there and give you a smack?"

"Hey!" I growled, glaring at the Potbellied Pig as I let the flames of my Dragon King burn brightly in my eyes. "What have I told you about threatening Violet?"

Refusing to look away or even so much as blink, I narrowed my eyes and waited, daring Bernie to speak. Silently counting, I got as far as three before the Cherub cursed to be a Potbellied Pig threw her front right hoof even higher in the air before slamming all four of her not-so dainty paws onto the rock floor and huffing, "Fine! Okay! Whatever! You deal with *her*." She pointed to Vi with the very tip of her little mauve snout. "Goddess knows, I've had enough."

Turning her very round, very pink body until she was facing me completely, she gave a bow with the bend of her right front leg then a snap of her head to the side. "Is it okay with you if I go stand over by that wall while you and the brain trust figure out our next move, oh Great and Wonderful Grand Poobah of all things Smoky and Scaly?"

"Bernie." It was Vi's turn to growl. "What is your problem? We're all in the same boat here…"

"It's a cave," Bernie scoffed, her hooves making a *tippity-tap, tippity-tap* as she traipsed to the far side of the cavern. "Not a boat, Violet. If it was a boat, I would've already abandoned ship."

"Whatever," Vi huffed. "You know what I mean. We should be working together to figure out where we are and how we got here instead of…"

"Instead of trying to find out if the God of Love has been turned into a mummy? I know Valentine's Day is already over, but we're gonna need him again. And what about Aphrodite – his Mommy Dearest. Are you gonna tell her that you left her baby boy in a cave covered in muck?" Bernie plopped her bodacious booty on the floor, let her head fall to the side, and harrumphed, "Hell, yes you are. 'Cause I'm damned sure not gonna be the messenger for that journey into the bowels of motherly love gone wrong." Throwing her hands in the air, she added, "But by all means, tell us what to do, Vi? What's your plan? How do we…"

"Oh, my great Lord of Hell, do you people ever shut up?"

The voice was tinny and nasally but somehow also had a deep resonance that sounded like the feedback from a speaker with the bass jacked up too high. Booming as if it was on surround sound, coming from every direction, the reverberating declaration echoed off the rocks, circled around itself and blasted right back in a continuous loop that bore into my brain, not unlike a jackhammer beating at concrete.

Holding on tight to my little Witch, I spun one way and then the other letting Esau's enhanced vision and preternatural senses search for our captor as the very same bastard taunted, "Where's the fear? The cowering? The begging for your lives? Has no one ever taught you to be victims? Why do you have to ruin everything? I've been planning this *forever!* Why are you people such... such... Assholes?!"

"I know that voice," Violet whispered directly into my mind, taking the words right out of my mouth.

"Me, too," I agreed *"But from where? We need to keep him talking."* Not waiting for an answer from Vi, I yelled aloud, "Show yourself. Come out and face me. You got us here. The least you can do is show us who you are and give us an explanation."

Listening to my own voice echoing through the vast tunnels of the underground labyrinth my Dragon King was quickly mapping, I was just about to demand again when a blast of Magic so black and so strong, not to mention, hideously noxious, hit me square in the chest like a pile of bricks fired out of a tennis ball launcher. Holding Violet as tight to my body as I could, just waiting for my back to hit the hard, cold rock behind me, another blast came careening from the opposite direction, and just like that my gorgeous Mate was ripped from my arms.

Flying one way as she flew the other, I roared, "VIO-LET!" at the same time that she yelled, "MICK!" Shockingly, Bernie also screamed, "VI! MICK! WHAT THE HELL?!"

Moving so fast the rocks on either side were nothing but a blur, my only concern was my Mate. The faster I flew, the fuzzier my vision became until I couldn't so much as see the nose on my face, much less where my little Witch had gone.

Was Violet okay? Why had she stopped yelling? What was happening and why wasn't Esau jumping into action and saving my ass as he had so many times before? Something was very, very wrong and I was very, very pissed.

"Old Man!" I yelled, waiting less than a second before

hollering again. *"Esau, you there? What's happening? Why aren't you...?"*

"I'm locked down tighter than Princess Periwinkle's chastity belt on Prom Night at the Fairy Mound. I got nothing. That last blast of..."

"Stop! Stop! Stop!" I bellowed, trying with every ounce of my own Magic, strength in my body, and prayer I'd ever prayed to halt my backward motion. I could feel the cold, sterile lifelessness of the granite wall right behind me and the doom it carried. I was about to be smooshed flatter than Lovebugs on a windshield in June and all I could do was roar, *"ESAU!"*

And that was all she wrote.

No time for a breath or a roar. Hell, I didn't even have time to tuck and roll. Instantly, everything became crystal clear as I was spun around more times than I could count like an ax thrown from a Berserker's hand at the Annual Supernatural Games and Fete.

Thankfully, I stopped a split-second before barfing up the egg sandwich and coffee I'd had for breakfast. Regrettably, I was facing forward and could now see where I was going. Trust me, knowing what's about to happen is not always all it's cracked up to be.

Hurdling headfirst towards a boulder rivaling the Rock of Gibraltar, I opened my mouth to tell Violet that I loved her one last time when the massive stone I was about to be irrevocably joined with started to shimmy and shake. Stretching and snapping back lengthways then from side-to-side, I swore I was looking in a funhouse mirror.

In and out of focus, the constant distortion making it hard for me to figure out which way was up, I opened my mouth to demand my captor stop this taunting bullshit, when the scent of rotten eggs, my brothers' dirty gym socks, and a heaping, steaming pile of good old fashioned horse shit filled my mouth, throat, and lungs. Sadly, I'd been inhaling when it happened, and there wasn't one damned thing I could do to stop the process. Not only was I going to become a fossil long before my time, but I was also going to gag to death on a scent worse than MacElfresh's Pig Farm in the middle of August.

No! None of this shit was on my bucket list. I was Dragon. Hear me roar. I was supposed to die on the battle-field, or better yet, in bed after making love to Violet for the hundred-millionth time. I was supposed to live to a ripe old age of a million-and-fifty-two with kids, and grandkids, and great-grandkids, and... oh, you get the picture.

Smashing into a big fucking rock after being kidnapped from Cloud Nine while visiting my Mate for the first time in more years than I wanted to think about had never been in the plan. It was utter bullshit, and I was pissed.

No, I was more than pissed. I was fit to be tied, flyin' off the handle, and so mad I could chew up nails and spit out a barbed wire fence. As soon as I got my hands on the bastard responsible for the mess we were in, I was going to rip off his left arm and beat him black and blue with it.

Which is why, I opened my mouth one more time despite the horrendous stench and snarled, "Bring it on, Asshole. Cats may have nine lives, but Dragons live forever. I'm gonna..."

Unfortunately, my big finish, my pièce de resistance was cut off, stopped short, and completely thwarted as I literally passed through seven feet of thick, gray and black sparkling granite, not unlike a drill bit through wood. Exiting the other side after what seemed like forever, I spit and sputtered and hacked up enough pebbles and dust to make a nice walkway through the garden at the Brown

Family Mansion. As if that wasn't enough, I coughed and hacked up sharp little pieces of shale and nuggets of geodes. There was absolutely no doubt that I resembled a goldfish spatting out the multi-colored rocks at the bottom of his tank.

Head bouncing off a pile of rocks, my left shoulder hit a stone ledge, my ass flew over my head, and in an embarrassing turn of events, I did what felt like the most awkward somersault ever rolled. Sliding ass over tea kettle across the gritty, grimy floor, I finally got onto my stomach, shoved the heels of my hands into the dirt beneath me, and used every ounce of muscle in every fiber of my being to come to a screeching halt.

Literally kissing the bottom step of a set of perfectly crafted, highly shined, and eerily glowing stairs, my eyes rolled upward and what I saw had me hissing, "Dip my balls in buttermilk and serve 'em with gravy, that's a fuckin' throne of skulls."

Springing to my feet while ignoring the fact that I felt like a piece of taffy fresh out of the puller, I could feel the power of Esau's Magic thrumming through my veins. The Old Guy was pissed and loaded for bear and any other time I would've sat back and watched the show. As happy as I was that our enchantment was back, there was nowhere to aim the fire, nobody to watch go up in flames.

We were alone. Or so I thought...

"You see anything, E?"

"If you don't see it," he growled. *"What makes you think I can? It's not like you're new here. We share a brain, a soul, a set of eyes."*

"Okay, Big Guy," I snarled right back. *"I know you're pissed. It's not like things are going the way I planned either. We need to figure out where we are, where Violet is, and..."*

"And how the hell we get from here to there and how we get back. Yeah, I got that. We share a brain, remember?"

Refusing to give in to the Dragon King's frustrated taunts, I started looking for Violet. Maybe she was there, and I just didn't see her – or feel her – or hear her heart beating in sync with mine.

The way I saw it, both of us had been caught in a wave of nasty Magic, it only stood to reason that we'd both gone in the same direction, right?

(Yeah, I was grasping at straws. It's part of my process. Don't get sassy.)

Crossing to the closest side of the cavern, I reached up as far as I could before slowly running my hands down the rock wall. Up and down, moving forward at a snail's pace, I could feel Esau's frustration and anger growing with every swipe of my hand until he finally spat, *"What, in the name of King Arthur's Excalibur, are you doing?"*

"I thought you knew everything. Aren't you the Amazing Kreskin? Can't you read my mind? After all, we share a brain. Figure it out. What am I doing? Twiddling my thumbs? Playing tiddlywinks? What the hell would you be doing if you were out here, and I was in there?"

Fists flying out to the sides, my temper getting the better of me, I snarled, *"Wouldn't you be looking for Vi? Trying to find our Mate? Wouldn't you need to know that she's okay? If not find her right this minute, figure a way out so you can find her? What would you...?"*

"I would do exactly what you're doing," he acquiesced, exhaustedly exhaling with such force that my mind's eye filled with smoke. *"You're right. I'm wrong. I lost my cool. I'm..."*

"Sorry?" I forced a chuckle I truly didn't feel. *"I believe the word you were lookin' for was sorry."*

"Don't push it, Young'un."

"I hear ya'. That's as good as I'm gonna get. If it makes ya' feel any better, I'm sorry, too." Huffing out a breath as I ran my fingers through my hair, I added, *"This whole Mate thing has me..."*

"All tied up in your underwear," Esau snorted. *"Yeah, I know. I can feel it and I don't blame you one little bit."* Exhaling another plume of smoke, this one clearing my mind better than anything else ever could, he went on, *"Violet's the real deal and we need to get you back to her sooner rather than later. Now, let's find the bastard who brought us here, kick his ass, save your girl, and get the hell outta Dodge."*

"You got it," I vowed aloud, Esau's brilliant bronze scales shimmering over my arms. "Let's get the hell outta..."

"To your left!" Esau roared.

But it was too late.

I was already flying upward. For the tiniest of moments, I felt like a marionette and was sorry for what those little wooden characters must've endured.

With Esau's words still ringing in my mind, my back was slammed into the ceiling and every last breath forced from my lungs as thick, black, leathery tentacles wrapped tightly around my arms, legs, and waist. Stuck like a rat in a trap, staring down at the floor, I roared, "Show yourself, you spineless bastard! Stop with the fuckin' parlor tricks and come out and face me like a man!"

Long tense seconds ticked by. The overwhelming scent of rotten eggs combined with the sharp, bitter reek of ammonia filled the cavern. Eyes watering and my throat closing, it felt like I was drowning in a vat of fertilizer. Panting through gritted teeth, refusing to inhale any more than I absolutely had to, my eyes were narrowed to the thinnest of slits when a shadow appeared in the farthest corner.

The grating squeal of rock shifting over rock shook the walls as an opening I hadn't yet found got bigger and taller. The shadow grew longer and wider as it slithered into the light.

Then I heard it - the pounding of thunderous hooves on stone and the thud of meaty fists hitting rock. Whatever was coming thought it could intimidate me. Wanted me to be scared, to cower, to shake like a little boy scared of the dark.

Fuck that. Mick Archer cowers for *no one*!

Vibrating with unspent rage and Magic, the anticipation of seeing the one who'd dared to endanger my Mate became a living, seething entity within me. Never had I been so furious. Never had I seen red or had I let the bloodlust of Esau's Warrior Dragon take hold – but then again, never had anyone dared to threaten Violet.

(Well, more than Bernie, but she's just a little, tubby, loveable bag of hot air.)

"Steady," Esau warned. *"I know that scent. I know..."*

"You know nothing!" The nasally whine shot through the cavern a split-second before the unmistakable, unbelievable, unimaginable sight of an honest to the Goddess Minotaur came into view.

(For real, I thought they were just an old wives' tale. Something parents told naughty little kids to make them behave.)

At least eleven feet tall, shoulders so wide they barely fit through the recently opened mouth of the cave it was the very pointed tips of the very long and ostentatiously curved horns jutting from his head that *almost* gave me pause. Sure, Esau had battle horns and ridge horns and huge skeletal talons that jutted from the ends of his wings, but I wasn't in his flying form or his Warrior form. I was just Mick. Impressive, as that might be, in my present form, I was basically a Magical human, and I knew that just would *not* do.

If I was to save Violet, I had to live, and being skewered might impede my progress. I had to get down, Shift, and kick some Minotaur ass. I had to keep my cool. I had to...

Be a dumbass and open my mouth before my brain was fully engaged and the very little bit of self-preservation that I actually possessed kicked into gear. "'Bout time you showed up, Asshole. What were you...?"

And that was as far as I got before the Minotaur lifted his head and I got a good look at his face. It was unbelievable, something out of a memory or more precisely, a nightmare.

The unmistakable round, coke-bottle glasses sitting atop the bridge of his extremely wide nose. The watery, almost wimpy, certainly bloodshot pale blue eyes. The sneer of a boy who thought he was smarter than everybody else but never got the chance to prove it because he never got any taller than four-feet-nine or weighed more than ninety-eight pounds dripping wet.

Blinking once, twice, three times, my mouth opened and closed just as many times before the Bull guffawed, "What's wrong, Cuz? Surprised to see me? Maybe you missed me? Thought I was dead? Thought I was a Null? Didn't even try to find me when I disappeared? Can't believe I have Magic? Thought you and your stupid brothers were the only ones with shit parents? Were sure you deserved a life, happiness, a *Mate* more than anyone else because you were robbed of your birthright?"

Strutting around, the tips of his extra large and unfortunately, in charge horns tearing strips out of the brand new red T-shirt Vi had given me for Valentine's Day right along with the flesh covering the taunt six-pack of my abs, I didn't even feel the pain. Wouldn't have known he was serrating my skin had my blood not been dripping on the floor below. I just couldn't believe my eyes. It couldn't be, could it? It wasn't, was it?

"Harvey?"

"Well, damn, Mick," the cousin I hadn't seen since we were knee-high to a grasshopper sarcastically chuckled. "Good to see you, too. Sorry, it has to be this way, but sometimes shit happens."

"But how are you…?"

"Here? Looking so good? Kicking your ass?" Harvey's guffawing taunts filled the cavern. "Damn, Dude, you're seriously dumber than a box of rocks."

Pushing his glasses back up his nose, the man – no, make that Minotaur – I remembered as a thin, gaunt, little boy who liked to set fire to ants with his many magnifying glasses, collect butterflies and pin them to boards, and who could explain the development of a cockroach nymph with way more detail than anybody ever needed to know, stopped just under my face and looked me in the eye. Shaking his head, Harvey Archer tsked, "Yes, I was a Null, just like my parents – who not unlike yours wanted Magic and Power more than they ever wanted to be good role models or a decent mom and dad, but that's where the similarities in our stories end. You see, I was…"

Stopping midsentence, his eyes followed a rather large, rather red drop of blood as it fell from the gaping hole in my stomach. Hand shooting out, he caught the droplet on his fingertips with the dexterity of a man who had learned how to expertly maneuver his girth.

Spreading my blood across his fingertips with the pad of his enormous thumb, Harvey once again threw back his head and while looking me right in the eye, ran all four of the tips of all four his fingers across his face. It was a threat, a promise of a slow death, as sure as I was hanging like a ragdoll from the ceiling of his lair.

"Stop the shit, Harvey. Get to the point," I spat. "I never did anything to you. Hell, I stood up for you, protected you. Let me..."

"You never did anything to me?" He roared, his meaty paws hammering into my stomach, punctuating his next words with absolute clarity. "You. Never. Did. *Anything*. For. Me. You. Left."

More punches, his knuckles crunching my ribs, shattering my sternum, making mincemeat of my sternum, his whole body expanded, grew, became even more massive as his final promise echoed through the cave, "And. For. That. You. Will Die."

PART III

I'M NOT A PRINCESS AND I DO NOT NEED SAVING, BUT...

BLESS HIS HEART FOR TRYIN'.

"Are you sure you're okay?"

"Yes, Bernice," I groaned her given name with the loudest of sighs as I rolled my eyes to hide how much it meant to me that she actually cared. To be clear, I *knew* Bernie loved me, and she *knew* I loved her. We'd been stuck together for longer than either of us cared to admit and not just because we had to be. I mean, she was way more than just a Familiar, she was Family.

(And if you tell her I admitted that out loud, I'll turn *you* into a Potbellied Pig in a red tutu.)

The best word I can think of to describe our relationship would be... umm, well, I would have to say 'sisterly'. To be clear, I have no sisters. It was a Brown Witch thing. We're all only children born to only children who were born to only children and so on and so on. It had something to do with the whole 'Brown Witches having a *special* place in the world' thing.

(But those Omnipotent Beings made sure we all had a shitload of cousins who were just like sisters in every possible way. They knew the importance of Family. So, I called the Brown Witches and the Powers That Be even a long time ago and moved on.)

As far as I can figure, those powerful Omnipotent Beings believed our 'jobs' – our Callings - what we were born to do – would always come with more danger than the average Witch faced. Now, I know to you being the Keeper of the Sacred Pumpkin or of the Christmas Star or of the Spark of Love or of the Flame of Hope or of the Joy of the World or all the other things my Aunties and cousins and I are responsible for sound like sweet gigs - like they're no big deal, but just think...

No, seriously, take a moment and ponder what would happen if the Spark of Love went out for just a single second. If all the adoration, affection, tenderness, and smooshy gooey goodness of the whole universe blinked from existence for even a fraction of a blip of time.

Scary, huh? Yeah, now you see what I'm dealing with...

So, anyway, I knew from having friends who had sisters – not from my own personal experience, mind you, but also from how my cousins and I interacted - that Bernie and I dealt with each other in pretty much the same manner siblings did. We argued and disagreed and generally picked on each other every chance we got – but just let a third party enter the picture and dare to say one bad word towards my pleasantly plump and perfectly pink Familiar. Well, that was when Super Duper Bitch Witch Violet came bursting on the scene.

(You see, Bernie was mine to fight with, pick at, and generally mess with twenty-four/seven, and I was hers – but no one else's. Somebody messes with my Bernie and there was hell to pay. Point blank. Period. Ya' feel me? Cool.

Now, where was I...)

Oh, yeah, I'd just finished rolling my eyes when good ole Bernie trotted over to me, stood up ON her hind legs, and grabbed both my hands with her crazy little, bright pink hooves. Pulling me down to her level, she looked first in one eye and then the other before giving me a single sharp nod and declaring, "Yep! You're good."

Letting go of me with such force that I stumbled backward and barely stayed upright, she gave one loud clap of her hooves then pointed at the lump of 'stuff' we believed to be Cupid. "Now, let's figure out if that's the Boss. I need to know if I'm gonna live to a ripe old age of two-million-and-three or if the Goddess of Love is gonna cut that shit short."

"But what about Mick?"

Side-eyeing me with more disgust than was absolutely necessary, she deadpanned, "Salamander Ass can take care of himself. He's a Dragon Guardsman for cripes' sake. We need to save both our asses and make sure that's not the Big Boss. I don't want to be..."

"...fodder for one of Aphrodite's bitch fits," I finished her thought, throwing my hands in the air. "Yeah, I got that before. You've made your position perfectly clear. You'd rather *I* get turned into a gorgeous red and pink greasy spot with great hair and gorgeous eyes on the floor of her Crystal Castle than you. Point taken." Throwing said hands out in front of me, the tips of my fingers pointing towards the pile of whatever I was now *absolutely* sure was *not* Cupid – aka the Big Boss – because he is, after all, a God and would've recovered long ago, I sighed, "Lead on, oh, Potbellied Pig of Perpetual Petulance. I'm pretty sure we're wasting our time, but far be it for me to stop your fun. Let's go see if..."

"Wait one minute, Witch Hazel." Stamping one of the hooves that was still on the floor, she slammed the front two on her waist and groused, "It's not that I want you to get bitch slapped by the wrath of a goddess either, it's just that..."

"Yeah, I know. I get where you're comin' from. No worries, Berns. I'm *pretty sure* you won't let anything too terrible happen to me," I nodded just to keep the conversation rolling so that I could go find my Mate. "Now, can we just get this over with, *pretty puhlease*? I can't feel Mick anymore." Tapping my temple with the tip of my index finger, I explained, "And after him being back in my brain for the last six weeks then having the sensation ripped away, I am kinda lost. Something really wrong is happenin' 'round here and I'm sick and tired of bein' the butt of the bad guy's sick jokes, ya' feel me?"

"Damn straight, Sista," Bernie emphatically huffed. "We are Beings of Love and Light, but an ass whoopin' is not outta the question."

"You know it."

Having a small portion of our Magic back after being without it and feeling helpless for the last little bit, instilled us both with what we Witches and Familiars like to call Mystical Muscles. (Think beer muscles – like when guys named Bubba and Theo suddenly think they can take on the world, kick all kinds of ass, draw an S on their raggedy old T-shirt and stop a speeding combine with one hand after a case of Pabst Blue Ribbon or a bottle of the cheapest tequila. Don't judge. I'm proud to say that hillbillies – the nice variety that were taught good manners and treat everybody with common courtesy - make up ninety-nine-point-nine percent of my Family. So, I know whereof I speak.)

Stepping forward, I imitated a pistol with the first two

fingers of my left hand – my 'spelling' fingers, so to speak – and pointed them at the lumpy mound of cobweb-covered. With my Magic still a little less than full strength and the little Witch in the back of my mind refusing to wake up after my less than stellar attempt to 'fix' our predicament, I was forced to whip up a Spell and pray the Mistress of Magic was listening.

(Who is the Mistress of Magic? Well, she is the second cousin three times removed of the Great Goddess herself and the one relative of our most benevolent Deity with the ability to put the *poof* in the *spoof* and the *whammy* in the *kablammy* when a Witch's Magic is not quite up to snuff. Now, she can't restore said mysticism or remove whatever might be blocking it, but she can give us an *enchanted kick* in the abracadabra when we need it *and* - this bit is the most important – we plan to use said Magical wallop for good and not evil.)

"Get off the shelf. Reveal yourself. Please don't be Cupid. Don't make me feel stu... *whoa! What the...? Harvey?*"

Thankfully, the Mistress of Magic was listening. Not-so-thankfully, her crazy cousin, Fate – the silly Trickster She can be – decided to throw a great, big old monkey wrench in my plan at precisely the *wrong* second.

(Think – All the planning in the world can't beat dumb luck and you'll get the picture in bright, vivid, technicolor.)

I couldn't believe my eyes. Like seriously, I was so shocked, I forgot to stop my spell – or worse yet, control where the hell it was headed. The sparks and mist and bubbles that the Mistress of Magic had bestowed upon me and were shooting out of my fingertips went absolutely, completely, and totally *ev-ery-where* as my hand flew to my chest, my eyes damned near fell outta my head, and I gasped with such gusto I almost passed out when I forgot to exhale.

Bouncing off every surface and making up some others as it zipped and zapped through the air, thank the Goddess for Bernie...

(I know. I was pretty sure I was *never* gonna utter those words either.)

...because she stepped right up and screamed a counter Spell at the top of her little pink lungs, "Stop this shit! I can't help that Vi's a dimwit. Cut the crap. Or I'll blow ya' off the whole damned map!"

(Yes, I taught Bernie to use Spells, too. I figured there would come a time I needed her to save my ass. And lookie here, I was right.)

Not sure my Pig's shrieked Spell would work, I ducked and searched for cover just in case I was about to become a greasy spot of my own creation. With no cover in sight and nowhere to run, I was bobbing and weaving long after I really had to, something I have on good authority confirmed I was the biggest goofball in the history of goofballs.

In retrospect, it did my heart good to know Bernie would save my ass from imminent demise should the need arise. And even better, I watched through one eye with my hands still over my head as her bout of benevolence didn't end there.

Shooting across the rocky room, all four of her little legs moving so fast they were nothing but a blur of bright pink and mauve, she scampered up the pile of crud we now knew was *not* Cupid, and jabbed Harvey Archer right in the chest.

"Who are you? Where did you come from? And why the hell did you put us down here?"

Looking through very black, very round, coke-bottle-lensed glasses, the wimpiest...

(Yes, I know it's a horrible thing to say about another person, but it was the only adjective that worked. No, really, I promise I'm not just being a brat. Here, let me paint you a picture and you can form your own opinion, m'kay?

Ya' know the skinny, awkward, nerdy kids you see in science class, comic books, or after school specials? The ones who have holsters for their inhalers that color coordinate with their pocket protectors and their briefcases? The ones who think it's cool to dissect frogs or create robotic girlfriends. Yeah, those guys – the next reclusive CEOs, billionaires, or owners of the major tech companies who couldn't carry on a conversation that didn't include the words – snot, allergies, and Dr. Weinstein – if their lives depended on it.

Well, Harvey Archer made all of them you've ever heard of look cooler than Don Juan and stronger than Superman. Sure, he was one of my Mick's many, many, many cousins and a Null, but he was also the only one I'd ever met who wasn't good-looking, smart, and muscled to the max, however, none of that negated the fact that he was creepy with a capital C.

Not creepy just because his IQ was so high he ruined every grading curve. No way. I am not that petty. I'm talking about the skeevy kinda creepy that made your skin crawl when he looked at me because it was obvious he was imagining what I looked like naked, or at the very least in my bra and panties. Can we all say, *Ewwww*?

Now, stop rolling your eyes, pursing your lips, and shaking your head as you think horrible, terrible, nasty thoughts about me. I swear I am not making it up. Every girl – Other or otherwise – had experienced the Harvey Stare. You can ask any of them. They'll back me up. Besides, you and I know each other well enough for you to be sure I will always tell you the truth – no matter how ugly it may be – and this time is no different.

So, here it is. My very own reason for thinking that Harvey Archer should've been named Tom... Like Peeping Tom, in case you didn't get my drift...

How would you feel about finding said nerd boy crouched outside your bedroom window, looking through binocular glasses he created in his very own home laboratory, as he snapped polaroids of your brand new teenage curves in your first ever matching bra and panty set?

Yeah, that's what I thought. You'd be as mad as a three-legged dog tryin' to bury a turd on an icy pond while having a hissy fit as you screamed, "Harvey Archer, you better give your heart to Jesus because your butt is mine."

Now, you know how I felt. And I wasn't the only girl – be they Witch or Other – to have experienced the slimy stalkery of Harvey Archer. There wasn't a female in Nowhere USA High School and Supernatural Academy who didn't run at the sound of his whispering wheezing, hide in the bathroom when his nasally voice screeched their name or was forced to whip up an Anti-Peeping Harvey Potion and slather it all over every window of their family home.

However - and I say that with an exasperated exhale and shake of my head – there was just something about me – Violet Elizabeth Brown, Brown Witch Extraordinaire and the Keeper of the Spark of Love that kept ol' Harvey coming back for more. No matter what I did, no matter how many times I asked nicely or turned him into a pink Toad or threatened to tell Mick, that that bespeckled ninety-eight-pound Null refused to give up.

Finally, when I was seventeen and deep in the throes of my hundredth serious crush on the one and only Mick

Archer, I lost my cool and told my Auntie Belinda about my 'pest problem'. Now, before you ask, the reason I never told her before that moment was because Auntie B was not known for her restraint and decorum and couldn't give a good gosh darn if Harvey Archer was the favorite nephew of Big Daddy and Mother Archer. Hell, she wouldn't have cared if the little creep was the nephew of the Goddess Herself.

And that is just one of the things I love about Auntie Belinda.

Never one to let me down, the coolest of all the aunties in the Brown Family Coven, Lindy – as she's known to her friends – jumped into action. With little more than a muttered, "I'll fix that little sneaky bastard's little red wagon. Bastard needs to keep those spooky spectacles to himself," she snapped her fingers, turned herself into an Owl, and promptly waited on the branch of the oak tree outside my window.

Sure enough, in less than an hour, the screams of a very scared, running-for-his-life Harvey Archer filled the evening air. The image of a feathered, screeching Lindy in Owl form chasing his skinny behind all the way back to his family's farm will forever be etched on my brain. Best of all, I'm happy to report that Peeping Harvey was no more, and the rest of my high school years were stalker free.

Heck, the girls of Nowhere USA High School and Supernatural Academy were so thankful, they changed the mascot to an Owl and made Auntie Lindy Head Teacher of Supernatural Shifting for Fun and Personal Safety. Now, do you see why I feel the way I do about Harvey Archer? Okay then. Thank you. Now, where was I?

Oh yeah...)

Watching my three-foot-two-inch, full of piss and vinegar, madder than a mule chewing bumblebees, very pink, very round, and red-tutu-wearing Familiar jabbing the substantially taller and definitely broader than I remembered Harvey Archer in the chest as she demanded answers, I almost jumped on the bandwagon and started yelling along. But something gave me pause. Whether it was the weird way he looked at Bernie like she was an amoeba on a flea's ass and he was the exterminator or the surly sneer that curled his lips, I'll never be sure, however, I thank the Goddess every day that the little Witch in the back of my mind chose that moment to wake up and whisper, *"Watch out, Vi. That one's up to no good."*

Deciding it was time to put up or shut up and figure out exactly what was going on, I tsked, "Oh, Bernie, stop being such a butthead." Adding a little shimmy to the sway of my hips, a fluttering bat of my eyes, I wiped the dust from my cheeks and fluffed my long brown curls while trying not to throw up and tittered like the twit he obviously thought me to be, "Be nice to Harvey. It's been..."

Giving the Nerd a wink as I crinkled my nose and giggled, I asked in an octave higher and goofier than I knew could be mustered from my sarcastic, curvy person, "How long *has* it been, Harvey? I think the last time I saw you..."

"Belinda Brown - aka the Screech Owl from Hell- was chasing me down the road trying to peck the hair off my head and the skin off my ass," he deadpanned, his aura doing a wonky swirly thing with muddy brown and inky black entering the mix.

"Something is seriously wrong with this idiot." Bernie's voice echoed through my brain at the same time that the voice of the little Witch in the back of my mind added, *"Things are not as they seem, Vi. You need to be careful."*

"Hush y'all," I sassed right back. *"I've got a plan."*

And with those fateful words and the groans of my Conscience and my Familiar I went in for the kill – so to speak...

Stopping just close enough to lay my hand on Harvey's upper arm and give it a lovin' (Well, pretend loving at least.) rub, I giggled like the idiot I most certainly was not. "I am so sorry 'bout that. Auntie Lindy could be ever so overprotective. I tried to stop her, really I did..."

(I was hoping I wouldn't go to Hell for lying. As you know, I was cheering her on like the Dallas Cowboy Cheerleaders in the last five seconds of the 1996 Super Bowl. Don't you think the Goddess would forgive me? I was, after all, doing it to try and find my hunka-hunka- burnin' love. She would do the same thing to save her Mate, right?)

"But she said you were climbing the tree outside my bedroom window with a camera in one hand and binoculars around your..."

"They're called Spectanoculars," he proudly corrected, shoulders rolling back, spine straightening, and his eyes glowing in the eeriest of ways. "My own invention, one I have patented, and I might add, is selling *very well* in the Asian markets."

(See? I told you he was that *kinda* nerd. His glasses even got a little steamy as he proudly touted his brainy accomplishment.)

"Oh, wow," I gasped, laying my free hand over my heart and leaning in just a little more as I feigned awe and batted my eyes. "I always told the other girls that you were gonna make it big someday."

"You did?" He growled, his bushy eyebrows furrowing so much they resembled a caterpillar sitting atop the nosepiece of his glasses. "Seriously? I always thought..."

"Oh, please," I tsked with a shake of my head and

another, more convincing pat on the arm as I got a little closer. "You have to know how much I always admired you. It's not like I tried to hide it or anything. It's just that Mick..."

"Mick was always in the way."

At his snarled response the scent of mesquite, and fresh air, and sexy male Dragon that I loved with all my heart filled my nose. *"I told you something was up with this buttbrain,"* Bernie hissed into my mind. *"Let me turn him into a worm, or a flea, or a speck of dust under Madam Misty's bed at the Best Little Whore House in Nowhere, USA."*

"No," I hissed. *"We have to..."*

But I was too late. There was no stopping Bernice the Beautiful, Bountiful, and Beloved. For all her blustering and taunting she loved Mick probably more than she loved me and she was not going to let Nerd Boy harm a scale on my Mate's sexy behind.

Racing past me at the speed of light – something I can tell you I had never seen before – Bernie launched herself into the air like a rocket shot out of a launcher. Bright red tutu flapping to give her extra propulsion and accurate aiming, she dropped her head to her chest and wailed, "You stupid, four-eyed, no good, rat bastard, if you've harmed a single hair on that Dragon's head, I swear to all that's... What the hell?!"

And just like that, I came as close to being literally shocked to death as I ever want to come. From one bat of my long eyelashes to the next, Harvey went from five-foot-eight and probably a hundred-and-fifty pounds...

(I told you he was bigger than the last time I saw him, although no matter of weight and height could stop him from still being kinda whiny and wimpy.)

...to an honest to the Goddess, real life, standing right in front of me Minotaur – and no, I am not exaggerating, embellishing, or pulling your leg in any way, shape or form.

Towering at least six feet over my rather lovely five-foot-five stature...

(Yep, that adds up to at least eleven-foot-five.)

...with a chest so wide an unpregnant Molly, a tiny Ella, and I could've camped out in the smooth, stiff, black-as-night fur...

(I have no clue how wide that is in inches or centimeters, just that it was at least as big as the floor of the pillow forts we used to build.)

...he had the head of a bull – massive, leathery nose with nostrils so big just one of them could've swallowed up my whole head - the body of the last three Mr. Universe's all mushed into one BIG guy...

(I swear, even old Arnold S. in his heyday would've looked like a baby chipmunk next to Minotaur Harvey.)

...his hands were so big they could've palmed three basketballs, and where his feet should've been there were hooves so huge Shaq's tennis shoes would've looked like baby booties next to them.

Taking all of that into account was daunting, to say the least, but it was the ginormous, long, thick, absolutely huge, curved, and carved horns jutting from his head that I know measured nothing short of twenty feet from tip to tip that scared the *witchy bejeezus* right out of me and had me screaming, "Pull back! Abort! Stop, Bernie! Stooooooooop!"

But it was not meant to be, and pretty much a waste of breath because as I was shrieking at the top of my lungs, Harvey - aka the Minotaur in the room – snatched my perfectly pink and precociously petulant Potbellied Pig right out of the air. Massive hand wrapped around her tummy, he held her over his head, shook my poor Bernie till her little black eyes bounced from side-to-side and roared, "You will be mine, Violet Brown! Mick will die! Big Daddy and Mother Archer will be avenged, and YOU WILL BE MINE!"

"Wait!" I roared, the sound reminding me more of Esau than the little Witch who lived inside of me. "What the hell did you just say?"

Up from my crouched position, hands flying off my head, I slammed one fist onto my hip as the index finger of the other snapped into a wagging position and I snarled, "Did you just have the utter nerve to mention those idiots?"

A step forward, my finger leading the way with blinding rage and burning Magic bringing up the rear, I continued to growl, "To me? The worst parents in the history of parents? The people who tried to kill my beloved cousin? Who wanted to steal all the Brown Family Magic? Who didn't give a good gosh darn about their boys or anyone else? The same..."

"Shut the fuck up, Violet!" Harvey roared, throwing Bernie like she was a football, he was the quarterback, and his team needed a Hail Mary as he bellowed, "I will have you! I will break you! I will..."

"You will eat shit and die!" Bernie hollered as the magically purple and perfectly pink sparkling rope shooting out of the finger that had once been wagging at Harvey wrapped around her tummy and pulled her to me. "I will turn you into a Toad and feed you to Gloria Gator. I will Magick your ass to the lowest Pit of Hell, coat you in the scent of tuna and catnip, and drop you in the kitty box of Lucifer's prettiest pussies. I will..."

"You will do nothing of the kind!" Harvey exploded, his voice like a giant foghorn as black smog, onyx fireworks, and the fetid stench of rotten eggs zipping and zapping from the tips of his horns. "Uncle Big Daddy and Auntie Mother Archer promised I could have you..."

Wham! Another crack of Magic hit the rocks right next to me just as Bernie's feet hit the ground. Diving in the opposite direction, I would like to tell you that I moved with the grace of a well-trained stunt woman, but sadly, I would be lying.

Slamming my hands into the stone floor so hard my body shimmied and shook so hard my eyes damned near rolled back in my head, I managed to barrel roll out of the way and get to my knees before Harvey fired off another round of noxious sorcery while continuing to rage, "...as long as I make Mick pay for turning on them. They promised!"

Acting like a very large, very pissed off sullen two-year-old who was about to take his toys and run home to momma, the nasally whine returned to Harvey's rumbling baritone making him sound as if the reverb on his internal sound system was all whacked out. "Those fucking Archer boys should've stayed gone. They got their Magic. They got their Dragons. They. Got. Everything!"

Arms extended to what looked like the length of half a football field, that crazy ass Minotaur lowered his head, rolled his eyes up as high as they would go, and glared at me as his eyes glowed an eerie bloodred and the black of his pupils overtook everything else. Tossing his head to and fro, his stance widened, and he pawed the ground.

I swear to the Great Goddess, I was waiting to hear the music of trumpets playing the Pasodoble and a matador's red cape to appear in my hands. Thankfully, it was Bernie's voice shouting in my brain that spurred me into action.

"Wake the hell up, Vi! That bullshit bull's about to charge!" The tippity-tap of her hooves on the rocks wiping away the

last of my shock, she barked, *"You go left! I'll go right! Let's wrap this mutha ducker up!"*

Acting without thinking, I did *exactly* as I was told for the first time in my very long life. Unfortunately, Harvey was in full Minotaur mode and moving damned near faster than my eyes could track. Twisting his torso and legs to the left as he kept his head and those long-ass horns pointed towards me, that rat bastard was making sure I could see exactly how big he truly was. Having the utter nerve to try and intimidate me. Who the hell did he think he was?

With a war cry that would've made Sitting Bull happy, I screamed, "Go straight back to hell, Harvey Archer," as I ran full speed to the left with Magic coming out of every orifice I could force it from.

Growling so low and with so much power that the ground beneath my feet shook and rocks and dust fell from the ceiling the Minotaur that was Harvey Archer audibly breathed, *"Rrrrumph rrrrumph,* you will be mine. *Rrrrumph rrrrumph,* Violet Brown!"

Dropping to my knees and sliding across the gravel and dirt to avoid a swipe of his mighty horns, I fired off a bolt of the harshest, nastiest Magic the Keeper of the Spark of Love could conjure. Literally hitting the Bull's eye – or rather, the Bull's belly – at exactly the same moment that Bernie crashed into his knees, all I could do was yell, "Timber!"

It was a thing of beauty, extreme hilarity, and the best sight I'd ever laid eyes on...

(Aside from seeing Mick for the first time in forever.)

...as Harvey's big ass hooves got tangled up in Bernie's tutu and in one fell-swoop a ginormous, gigantic, giant pain in the ass Minotaur flew ass over tits through the air. In the blink of an eye, everything seemed to switch to slow motion and it was the best show I'd ever seen.

Mouth open so wide he could've swallowed both of his big, clopping hooves...

(Talk about hoof-in-mouth disease, that Minotaur had a case not even Dr. Bombay could cure.)

...Harvey's terrified roars echoed and reverberated until my ears were ringing so loud I barely heard Bernie shriek, "Shut the hell up, Asshole! Take your payback with a bit of dignity!"

Slamming into a very huge, very pointed rock sticking out of the farthest wall, Harvey's cries cut out like someone had flipped a switch. Jumping to my feet, I was just about to blast him again, when the nerdiest jackass to ever walk the planet crumbled into a massive pile of mangy Minotaur hide and big curvy horns with stupid, round coke-bottle-lensed glasses hanging from one of his ears.

And just like that, the rest of my Magic – and Bernie's, too – came whooshing back in a cloud of wonderful red bubbles, pink sparkles, and beautiful lavender mist. With only a look and a wink between us, my Potbellied Familiar and I lifted our hands and let the Mysticism flow.

Wrapping Harvey up as tight as we could in enchanted ropes, charmed shackles, and a chain imbued with so much Magic I knew only the Great Goddess Herself could break the links, I turned towards Bernie and got as far as, "Damn, Girl, we make one helluva a te..."

When Mick raced into the room looking like he'd been through one too many spin cycles in an industrial washing machine filled with nuts and bolts. Shirt torn to shreds, blood stains covering most of his wonderfully and perma-nently tanned skin, he was winded and heaving as his eyes flew from my face to Bernie and finally to a trussed-up, still unconscious Harvey.

Throwing his hands in the air, my man, my Dragon, my

hunka-hunka-burnin' love huffed, "Well, shit, you don't need me at all, do ya'?"

"Nope," Bernie scoffed.

To which I growled, "Bernice," while goosing her good with a zipping zap of Magic.

Running across the dingy cave and into the waiting arms of my Mate, I wrapped my arms around his neck, planted a big kiss on his lips, and reassured straight into his mind, *I'll always need you, Mick Archer, forever and ever, Amen and then some.*

PART IV

BACK ON CLOUD NINE...

FOR NOW, ANYWAY...

"Okay, I get that Harvey is now in Hell with your mom and dad, but how did he get to be a Minotaur?" Bernie asked for the umpteenth time.

"He made a deal with one of the big-horned freaks," Vi harrumphed, entering the living room with a plate of cookies and a pot of her amazing hazelnut coffee lattes. "How many times have we explained this to you? He was crazier than a bedbug, nuttier than a squirrel turd, seventeen bricks shy of a load, his ducks do not waddle in a row. How many more ways can I say it?"

"A hundred," Bernie sassed right back. "And it still won't make a damned bit of sense. Minotaurs are born, not made." Pounding her fist - because she was back to being her normal three-foot-three-inch Cherub self since we were once again in the Kingdom of Love – on a very big, absolutely ancient volume of the History of Supernatural Beings, my wonderful, amazing, and terrific Mate's Familiar went on, "So, how the hell did geek butt extraordinaire Harvey

Archer go from the ninety-eight-pound-dripping-wet weak-ling y'all say he was to that big ass Bull-with-an-attitude-problem we delivered to the Authority? It just doesn't add up. And, while we're at it, how in all the heck and honannies did he communicate with your mom and dad, Gecko Ass? *You said*, that Big Daddy and Mother Archer are locked down tighter than two-ton Tony's thighs in his fluorescent yellow spandex shorts. They don't even get to speak to the Demons who guard the gates to Satan's Cats' kitty boxes as they scoop the shit. How would Harvey have known what happened? That you and your brothers were the reason his beloved aunt and uncle were incarcerated in the most heinous, however befitting, way possible? And furthermore..."

"Furthermore," Cupid interrupted with a sarcastic chuckle as he appeared out of thin air in the middle of Vi's living room. "You ask too many damned questions, Bernice - always have and always will"

"Yeah, well, you don't give enough answers, Kewpie Doll, but that doesn't stop you from talkin'."

"Bernice!" Vi and I spat in unison with my gorgeous little Witch adding, "When will you ever learn? Do you want to be turned into a Potbellied Pig for all time – *everywhere*? Keep your trap shut. Show some respect. Think before you..."

"Oh, bite my ass," Bernie grumped, crossing her chubby little arms over her chest and pouting better than anyone I'd ever seen. "Can I help it that I was born with a brain? That I want answers? That I...?"

"Never know when to shut up?" Cupid dared, his blond eyebrows disappearing under his curly bangs and he glared at the Cherub with eyes so wide they looked a whole helluva lot like blue and white marbles.

Long tense seconds ticked by. Neither Bernie nor the God of Love was about to give in, look away, or so much as blink. It was a true stand-off, and I admit, I was having a good time watching it all unfold.

However, Violet was not.

"Okay, y'all, I've had about all the bickering and fighting I can stand for a millennium or two. Either you make up and play nice, or Mick and I are going back to Nowhere, USA *alone and for the rest of all time.*"

"You wouldn't dare!" Bernie and Cupid spat in unison, both of their heads snapping towards my little Witch, both sets of bright blue eyes as big and round as saucers and both jaws damned near dragging the ground.

Making a show of smoothing her cute little pink skirt, the love of my life, sat down on my lap, wrapped an arm around my neck, and nodded, "Oh, yes we will unless you two stop your constant bitchin' and get along."

"Okay, alright, you win," Bernie hastily agreed, her white-blond curls flying in every direction as she furiously nodded. With a sideways snap of her head, she added, "I'll be good if he will."

"I am the God of Love and what I say..."

"Okay, fine," Vi sniffed, the twinkle in her eyes telling me that she was having way too much fun at Cupid and Bernie's expense and loving every minute of it. Holding up her free hand, her thumb and fingers poised for the all-important Magical snap, she tsked, "If you won't even try, then I guess this is goodb..."

"Okay, okay, okay," Cupid relented, his lips turned down and the scent of cinnamon filling the air. "I'll try to be nice, but if she so much as..."

Hand going higher, Vi slowly shook her head. "No qualifiers. No if's, and's, or but's. Got it, Big Guy?"

"Yeah, I got it," Cupid groaned, the roll of his eyes so comical I had to bite the insides of my cheeks to keep from laughing out loud. Not only was my Mate the best Witch in the whole damned universe, but she also had the God of Love wrapped around her little finger. Violet Elizabeth Brown – soon-to-be Archer was nothing short of fan-fucking-tastic and best of all, she was all mine.

"Now, why are you here?" She asked Cupid before pointing at the food on the table and adding, "Want some cookies and latte? Or I can whip you up one of my famous and delicious strawberry shakes, if you're in the mood."

"Nope, I'm good. Krissy is fixing dinner and it's my turn to bathe the kids. I just wanted to stop by and give you the news from Hades." Handing Violet a red envelope, he nodded, "Aunt Persephone finally got back to me. I wrote it all down, but the Reader's Digest version is that the Archer's made friends with one of their Demon guards and convinced him to reach out to Harvey."

"How the hell...?" I hissed.

Holding up his hand, Cupid nodded in my direction and kept right on going, "Apparently, they knew all along that Harvey's parents bartered him to a Herd of Minotaurs in exchange for a talisman of Magic. Of course, it was all a double-cross. The Minotaurs killed Harvey's parents on the spot, took your cousin, and raised him as a Shifter – the only one of their Herd who could mingle with humans or Others and not be suspected of being anything other than a Null."

"I had no clue Minotaurs had that kind of Magic," Bernie mused. "Never heard of them being anything but big bullies, the muscle and brawn almost always controlled by somebody else."

"Yeah," I agreed. "I mean, first of all, I'm sorry that happened to Harvey, but I wasn't there. It's not my fault or my brothers. And, as far as I know, mom and dad didn't do a damned thing to help him or look for him. Hell, they probably didn't even miss him." Shaking my head, I sighed, "Well, anyhow, he's locked away and can't hurt anyone else. Secondly, and more importantly, there's a very small Herd of Minotaurs on the Isle of Skye, but their numbers are small, and they've taken the blood oath of Guardians. Chris checked all the records of the ancient Dragons and that specific Herd and its Alpha Bull have been allies of our kin for centuries."

"Well, you might want to give them a shout and let 'em know about the assholes in and around Nowhere, USA, I have no clue if they'll retaliate for Harvey's incarceration, but I don't think you should take any chances."

"You got it," I agreed. "I'll get on the horn to granddad and let him know."

"Okay," Cupid nodded as he blinked from view. "Talk to y'all later."

Pulling Violet close, I looked over her shoulder, met Bernie's eyes, and mouthed, "Scram."

True to form, the ill-tempered Cherub who loved my Mate like a sister, got to her feet as she grumbled, "Oh, hell yeah, I'll scram. I can't take any more of y'all's kissy-face, lovey-dovey bullshit. I'm getting a toothache and that's coming from a Cherub who lives on sweet tarts and candy hearts."

Snapping her fingers and Magicking out of sight, she added with a disembodied sigh, "I guess I love y'all, but don't let it go to your head. And I'll be back in the next day or two so get that crazy mooney-eyed crap outta your systems."

Looking down into the eyes of my little Witch, all I wanted to do was love her for all time, but of course, she had to ask for what seemed like the millionth time, "Are you sure you're okay with staying here for a while? With not being back at home with your brothers?"

Holding her close as I got to my feet and headed towards the stairs, I reassured my Mate with a cocksure grin and a wily wink. "As long as I am with you, I'm better than okay, *Mo ghrá*."

Snapping her fingers at the same time the ball of my right boot hit the bottom step, Violet waggled her eyebrows and gave me a husky whisper. "Then let the lovin' begin."

Whisked up the stairs, into what had become our room, and out of my clothes on a cloud of Magic and whole lotta love, I didn't even let my little Witch's feet touch the floor. Laying her in the middle of the bed, I followed her down, not willing to wait for another second to make the love to the only woman in the whole damned universe I'd ever loved.

Pulling back, I was just about to declare my undying love and devotion for the rest of forever when Vi beat me to the punch. Laying her hands on either side of my face, she looked me right in the eye and made no bones about it. "I love you, Michael Alexander Archer. I love you more than chocolate-covered cherries, more than red hearts and pink balloons, more than Valentine's Day, and more than being the Keeper of the Spark of Love. I've loved you since I was a little girl. I'll love you when I'm old. And when we both head up to the Heavens, well, I'm still gonna love you then, too. I need you more than I need to make sure Cupid and his army of Cherubs spread Amore all over the world and I'm prayin' with my whole heart that you'll make me the happiest Brown Witch ever and be my Mate forever and ever, Amen."

"Hey!" I griped, trying to act irritated and not grin from

ear-to-ear like the lovesick Dragon I was. "I thought I was supposed to do the asking."

"Nope," she corrected. "This is the twenty-first century, Bub and I ask for what I want and that, Mr. Archer, is you."

"Oh, hell, yeah," I whooped. "'Cause, you Mrs. Archer, are all I need."

Moving towards me at the same time that I reached for her, Vi's thigh rubbed my already throbbing erection and every thought of anything but making love to my little Witch flew from my brain. My hands couldn't - *no* - wouldn't stay still. I needed to touch her everywhere, needed to mark her with my scent, needed to be sure there was no way she would ever be anywhere but by my side. I'd been without her for too long, then to almost lose her in that damned cave after being with her for just six short weeks, well, that shit was never going to happen again.

Unable to hold back my shivers or the deep growl of her name when my little Witch slid the back of her hand across my chest, I slid my hand between our bodies loving the goosebumps that jumped to attention on her porcelain skin. Running the tips of my fingers through the damp curls covering her pussy, I lavished her beautiful, full breasts with kisses until I could take no more. Pulling as much of her heated flesh into my mouth as would fit, I sucked her hardened nipple between my lengthened canines, licking and teasing as my fingers slid closer to her throbbing clit.

Letting go, knowing before she did that Violet was about to pull away, I was in awe, lost in her lust-soaked eyes, the words, "I need to be inside you. I need you, Violet. I need you more than I need my next breath," tumbled from my lips.

And then as if my prayers had been answered, she gasped, "Yes...oh my, Goddess, yes, Mick. I need you."

Loving the feel of her nails digging into my shoulders, I couldn't help but be spurred on as my one and only love held on tight. Rolling to the side, balancing all my weight on one hand, I ever so slowly ran the other up the inside of her thigh.

Letting my hands go right back to where they'd left off, I leaned my forehead to Vi's, falling deeper in love with every beat of our hearts as I slipped first one and then another finger inside her waiting pussy. "Oh, Violet, *m 'ionmhas*, you're so wet, so ready, so needy for me. I want to have your taste on my tongue, but that'll just have to wait. If I'm not making love to you in the next little bit, I'm gonna lose my mind."

Working my digits in and out of her slick pussy, I couldn't look anywhere but deep into her eyes as the pad of my thumb finally teased her swollen, throbbing clit. "Come for me, Violet. Scream my name. Wet my hand. Come, *Mo ghrá*. I need to feel you come undone in my arms."

As the last word crossed my lips, I squeezed her clit between my thumb and forefinger and whispered, "I love you with all my heart, Violet Archer. Today, tomorrow, and forever."

Watching my Mate fly into orbit, scream until her throat was raw, and her eyes were glazed over with the passion of a well-loved woman, I knew if I died in that very moment, it would be as one truly happy Dragon. Unable to hold back any longer, I kissed her lips with all the hunger and fire I had only ever felt and only ever *would feel* for the one and only Violet Brown-Archer. Slowly pulling my fingers from her still quaking body, it took little more than a sensual roll of my hips, for me to slide just the tip of my cock inside my miraculous Mate.

Rolling my hips, following her amazingly erotic rhythm,

I never wanted our lovemaking to end. Being with Violet was like nothing I'd ever before felt. Every time was better than the last, just like the first, and without a doubt better than a trip to Heaven and a big, old, medium-rare T-bone all at the same time.

Raising my head, needing to look upon her, it was she who captured me with her mesmerizing gaze as inch by glorious inch, I slowly pushed into her wondrous body. Filling her so completely that I had no idea where she ended and I began, the earth stopped on its axis, my life was affirmed, and nothing that had come before mattered in the slightest.

Then she wrapped her legs around my waist, pulled me close, and I slipped even farther into the Heaven that was my Mate. Gasping, my heart skipping a beat, I could see the golden glow of the eyes of my Dragon illuminating the entire room. began to glow.

"I love you, Violet Elizabeth Brown-Archer. I love you more than I ever knew it was possible to love another person. I love you more than all the stars in the sky, and maybe by our two-hundredth anniversary, I'll find a better way to say it, but until then, I promise to try every day, in every way to make sure that you never have a single second's doubt how very much I adore you."

Pulling almost all the way out of her body, loving that she moaned at the loss and fought to keep me within her, I held still for less than a second before driving back into her pussy with wild abandon. Creating a frantic rhythm, more wonderful with each powerful thrust, my brains were scrambled, all rational thought was impossible and the fact that Vi was right there with me made it all more perfect.

With our minds as connected as our bodies, I knew the exact moment that she truly let go and loved me like there was no tomorrow. Her hips thrust against mine. Her fingers dove into my hair, and as she fisted the curls she refused to let me cut, the feel of her heated flesh against mine made it damned near impossible for me to hold off, waiting for her to come again. Needing her to know that her pleasure, her needs, her desires would always come first.

"M-Mick..." she stammered. "I n-need... I need... I nee..."

"What was that, my beautiful Witch? Did you say something?"

Yes, I was teasing, but I just couldn't help myself. Seeing my Mate in the throes of a passion only I could give her was better than flying, breathing fire, and delivering my asshole cousin to the Authority. It was pure bliss and I was going to enjoy every second.

Sure, I could read her thoughts, hear them screaming in my mind, but I needed Violet to say the words. Needed to hear the words tumbling from her lips. Slowing my thrusts, I purred, "Say it, Baby, tell me what you want."

"You, Mick Archer. You're all I want, all I need. For the millionth time, mark me as your very own."

Smiling with untold male pride, I went right back to the fantastic rhythm that only Violet and I could create. The one that made our hearts sing, our souls happy, and our bodies hum.

Kissing down her neck, I licked my Mate's pounding pulse, and whispered directly into her mind, *"I love you, Violet Brown-Archer, from this moment forward for the rest of all time, we shall be one."*

Sucking Vi's flesh between my teeth, I bit down so hard and fast, making sure she felt nothing but overwhelming pleasure and the timeless love of the man created for her by the Universe. The fiery thrill of love and passion tore through every fiber of my being, through her being, through our joined hearts, minds, and bodies, making us both whole for the very first time in our very long lives.

Screaming her release, the Magic of my bite solidifying the bond we'd always shared, Vi's body clenched mine and I was helpless but to follow her into the bliss of our love. It was as close to Heaven as I had ever been, and as I floated back to earth with my Mate in my arms, I planned to never leave our bed again.

Hours later and after many hours of lovemaking, Vi and I were blissfully happy being cuddled up together, the beat of our hearts the only sound we needed. Nothing ever had or ever would compare to the feeling of having someone I belonged to and who belonged to me.

"I have a present for you."

Raising her head and shoving my hair out of the way, Vi chuckled, "More than you've already given me?"

Barking with laughter, I snorted, "That wasn't a present, my love. That was a necessity and something I plan to repeat multiple times every day of our lives together."

Cocking an eyebrow, my sassy little Witch teased, "Multiple times a day? Can that go into double digits?"

Attacking her neck with pretend snarls and growls, I mercilessly tickled Vi's ribs until she was squealing, "Okay, okay, I give. You're the boss. You pick the number."

Stopping my pretend assault, I waggled my eyebrows, gave my Mate a quick kiss, and teased right back, "I get to be the Boss? Seriously? When did that shit happen? Can I get it in writing? Are you sure Bernie will agree?"

Patting my chest and rolling her eyes Vi groaned, "Bernie doesn't get a say in the matter, and no way in hell are you ever getting that shit in writing."

Moving as fast as Esau's speed would carry us, I rolled

Violet onto her back and kissed my little Witch until she was once again breathless, starry-eyed, and looking like a woman well-loved. Pulling back way before things got out of hand all over again, I rolled to the side with Violet along for the ride, stopping only when we were face-to-face with her left hand in my right one.

Feeling her falling deeper into my gaze, I slipped the ring on her finger and smiled so wide my cheeks hurt as Violet gasped, "What the...? For me? How did you...? Son of a Cherub without hearts on his diaper, I'm gonna cry."

Frantically shaking my head, knowing her tears would completely break my heart, I begged, "Happy tears, right?"

Eyes bouncing between mine and the biggest princess cut ruby set in platinum and diamonds I could find in and around the Isle of Skye, my sexy little Witch closed the distance between us. Pressing her lips to mine, she whispered directly into my mind, *"Of course, they're happy tears, Dragon Man. I've got you, haven't I?"*

"You bet your sweet ass, Mrs. Archer. You are stuck with me for-ever. And keep those tears to the happy variety, 'cause the sad tears will gut me for sure. I couldn't stand to be the cause of your pain. I will move Heaven and Earth to make sure you stay happy and smiling, my love." As our kiss grew more passionate, our legs tangled, and our bodies were once again heated with love and passion, Violet sighed blissfully, and I knew everything would always be okay.

One more time, just as I was sure it would always be, I needed what only my little Witch could give me. Crawling up my body, she pulled back from our kiss and looked down at me like I hung the moon and stars. Her happiness filled my soul and once again, I knew Violet Elizabeth Brown-Archer was made just for me.

Putting my hands around her waist, I sat up, kept Vi on

my lap, and kissed down her lovely neck, my erection growing hard between us letting her know I wanted her more with every passing minute. But my Mate had other things in mind.

Grabbing my shoulders, she pushed me back, looked me right in the eye, and shook her head with the authority of a woman who knows what she wants and how to get it. "Oh no, big guy. This time, I'll be the one doing the biting."

"Now, that's what I like to hear. Show me the way to Heaven, Sweetheart," I growled, rolling my hips against hers, teasing her already wet center, my fingers tangled in her hair as goosebumps danced up and down her spine.

Stopping for half a second, Violet asked, "How long was that ring burning a hole in your pocket, Dragon Man?"

"Since the day before I left the Isle of Skye, Witchy Poo."

Happy when she laid her lips back to mine, I couldn't help but chuckle as my sassy little Witch purred, "Good answer, Dragon Man. Less of the Witchy Poo shit, but good thinkin' with the ring."

Until we meet again...
Love always finds away.

JOIN THE CLAN!

Wanna keep up with all my crazy? Have fun? Win some cool prizes? Get *exclusive* excerpts to upcoming books? Sign up for my newsletter RIGHT HERE!

Be the FIRST to see new covers, sneak peeks, and best of all, ADVANCED COPIES OF ALL MY BOOKS!!!
Join the group! Julia's Mills' Fan Club on Facebook!

I absolutely LOVE stalkers! Here's all the links! Follow me everywhere!
Newsletter
Website
Facebook
Instagram
Twitter
Pinterest
BookBub
Goodreads

CHECK IT OUT!

A Sneak Peek of
DRAGONS FALL HARD
Book 3 ~ Dragon Guard Holiday Love Stories
Chapter One

"You better get naked."

"I *am* naked."

"A sports bra and yoga pants do not make a naked Witch."

"Oh, *puhlease* knock it off with the medieval boocrap, *Ollie!*" Moving my hands up and down my curvaceous physique, I kept right on going with the hopes that he would shut the hell up and pretend to be a statue. "This is as nekkid as I'm gonna get, *Ollie.* (Yep, I said it again for added irritation to the supreme butthead of all buttheads.) There is no way...."

"Do *not* call me Ollie."

The most miniature ball of feathers and BS - (Which stands for birdshit, not bullshit because, well, Ollie *is* a bird, as you will soon find out no matter how hard I try to act as if he does not exist.) - ever to be created growled with such fervor that his little body shook and tufts of down flew in every direction – including up my nose and down the front of my sports bra and into my cleavage.

"How many times do I have to...?"

"Ollie. Ollie. Ooooooollllllliiiieeeeeee!"

"Shut up, *Davina!*"

Singing at the top of my lungs, I added a booty shake, some jazz hands, a sneeze because there were tiny feathers in my nasal passages, and kept right on going – because, well, that big-eyed bugger was *not* the boss of me. Yes, I was attached to him like the chocolate on a cordial cherry because the Great Goddess and the Universe willed it to be so, but that didn't mean I had to like it – or be nice to him. (Okay, so I was probably supposed to be nice to him, and for the most part, I was. - sometimes. The Powers That Be didn't make mistakes, or so I had been repeatedly told but did not completely buy into based on the chaos that had always been my life. So, having said all that, I was forced to admit the cuckoo-for-cocoa-puffs ball of feathers and faffery was my Familiar, and it was my mission to drive him as bonkers as he drove me.

(I might be a bit spiteful and somewhat of a hand full. But I'm admitting this to you – and *only you.* If you tell anyone, I will ADAMANTLY deny it and turn you into a toad. Then you will be forced to bump your ass on the ground everywhere you care to travel, and everyone who knows you will point and laugh. Got it? Good.)

"Oh, Ollie, Ollie, Ollie, Ollie F. Plumage. Sometimes your breath smells like sewage. You...."

"My breath does not smell like...."

"...eat scorpions and grasshoppers. And even gecko

poppers. Sometimes I want to bop you. But mostly I want to... *arrrrghhhhhh!!!"*

Completely freaked out at the sight of my Familiar, one Oliver F. Plumage –

(Can you believe he *chose* that name? I know. I know. It's the worst. I mean, you would think he would've wanted something with more... Ummmm... I don't know, *panache*? How many people, owls, animals, birds, and/or *creatures* in this big blue and green ball we call home get to pick their very own name? No one! That's who. Well, no one *except* a handful of Familiars who were created by the Great Goddess and the Universe with the express purpose of being sidekicks to the one and only Brown Family Witches – which I happen to be. But, whatever, I digress. I have to admit that the moniker suits the little feathered fartface in all the right ways. So, just like momma said, all the planning in the world can't beat dumb luck – not even if you're the Great Goddess giving a Familiar his choice of names. Ha!)

Now, where was I? Oh, yeah....

Completely freaked out at the sight of my Familiar, one Oliver F. Plumage, careening towards me at a high rate of speed with the talons from his back legs so far out in front of his booty they were all I could see, I screamed like a little girl in a candy store that just ran out of orange gummy bears because I was scared all the way down to my skivvies....

(Yes, I was wearing underwear under my yoga pants. Geez. Get your mind outta the gutter. I've got serious junk in my trunk that needs to be restrained when out in public – or the wilderness, or pretty much anywhere but the comfort of my own home - and panty lines do not bother me in the slightest. Ya' know what I mean?)

Okay, let's try this again.

As terrified as Dr. Bombay was when the one and only

amazingly wonderful Witchy Physician was forced to deliver Medusa's quadruplets without the benefit of Magical drugs and sunglasses as that blasted winged weasel - the smallest and oldest living Elf Owl in all the world - who also happened to be the most annoying Sidekick in that *same* universe, came flying towards me at the speed of light....

(Or feathers or as fast as the remote-controlled airplane I turned into the tiniest supersonic Learjet ever to be Magicked for Ollie's thousandth birthday so he could keep up with me - whichever paints the right picture for you. I'm really easy to work with. Honestly, I'm one of the sweetest people you'll ever know if I do say so myself. I just happen to be incredibly reactive and, as stated before – a little bit of a handful.)

Okay, this time I promise to finish this part of my story....

More scared than I'd ever been as Ollie flew at me with a murderous intent shining in his huge chocolate brown eyes that could not be ignored, I was unable to finish my silly - yet perfectly crafted song. Instead, and much to my chagrin, I was forced to scream my terror at the top of my lungs for all who happened to be within shrieking distance of *Sgùrr Alasdair*, the highest peak of the Black Cuillin Mountains, on the Isle of Skye, in the Inner Hebrides, and indeed in all the Scottish Islands to hear.

(Yes, that was your geography lesson for today. I have an Auntie who insists we learn something new every day, and I am sharing my knowledge with you. Also, without a doubt, I will get to the reason why I was so far from home in just a minute.)

Unable to move nary a muscle - even as the little Witch in my head shrieked, *"Move your cute little ass, Davina Elizabeth Brown,"* - all the air in my lungs made a hasty exit when one-point-four pounds and nine whole inches of fluff, feathers, and foolhardy fuckery hit me in the chest with the force of a full grown, fifteen-thousand-pound bull elephant.

(Nope, no newborn calf for me, no way, no how and an oh, hell no for good measure. That goofy little bird of prey felt like a full-sized baby elephant who had devoured three tons too many peanuts and was retaining a metric ton of water caused by ingesting way too much salt from said peanuts. Think Pachyderm with a capital P.)

As a result of the Owl-who's-name-shall-not-be-uttered-at-this-time but will instead be called anything and everything under the sun but his given name pouncing on me like a Cheetah in heat....

My ass hit the ground. My back joined the party. And only by the grace of the Great Goddess herself did my head keep from doing all of the above and then some, which most definitely would have resulted in a Witchy concussion and inventive curse words flying from my mouth at a high rate of speed.

Now, you would think the little rat with wings would've stopped there – but he did not.

Landing on my chest, he proudly plopped his feathered behind in the very center of my well-endowed, double-d cleavage with a gleam in his eyes that meant he was nowhere near finished. Then, to add insult to injury, that wicked little Elf Owl whipped his wings to the front, slapped them onto both sides of my face, and glared at me with homicidal resolve burning in the tips of every one of his brown, black, tawny, and white feathers. Then, growling like a tiger a hundred times his size, he spat, "My. Name. Is. Not. Ollie."

Yes, at this point, I should've kept my mouth shut. Absolutely, I should've zipped my lips up tight. Of course, it would've been incredibly prudent to click the lock into place and throw away the key.

But... I did not.

Instead, I firmly but gently - because I would not have enjoyed having my eyes pecked out by the most miniature Owl to ever sprout wings and take to the sky - wrapped my hands around Ollie's tiny body and gave him a little shake. Then with the care some people give to moving crystal that belonged to the late Queen of England from one shelf to another, I lifted my fart-faced Familiar off my chest and gingerly deposited his butt on a lush, thick patch of weeds that just happened to be right next to my head.

(Now, I will admit to you – yes, *only* you – that my self-preservation and goodwill ended there. For in that moment, I wished for poison oak, poison ivy, poison sumac, and every other poisonous foliage known to man and the Great Goddess to be mixed in with those lovely weeds, heather, and assorted mosses and grasses. Oh! And let us not forget that I literally prayed to all The Powers That Be for long, pointy thorns to poke Ollie in the booty and fire ants to bite him in all the right - and wrong - places where the sun did not dare to shine. Suffice it to say, *none* of that happened. But, also, and this is the important part, I *still* tried to wish all of the above into existence, and that has to count for something.)

Forcing myself into a sitting position, I straightened the messy bun atop my head, adjusted my sports bra to avoid a wardrobe malfunction, and swiveled on my butt to face the very same bane of my existence. Looking at him with all the piss, vinegar, and rage an almost two-hundred-year-old Brown Witch can muster, I inhaled sharply through my nose, then exhaled through what I hoped still remained of my *Perfect Peach* MAC lip gloss.

"Was that absolutely necessary?"

Narrowing his left eye as he arched his right eyebrow, Ollie the Awful looked at me with all the haughtiness of a really, really, *really* old Magical Being and seethed through gritted teeth, "Yes, as a matter of fact, it was."

Jumping to my feet as fast as my curvy physique and well-rounded booty would allow, I slammed my fists onto my hips, bent at my waist, and refused to look anywhere but straight into his black soul. "Look, Bub, it is your fault that we're here, atop *Mount Scooterloaf Alexander....*"

"*Sgùrr Alasdair,*" Ollie the Butthead sighed. "Your Gaelic is...."

"Perfect," I seethed. "So shut it." Sticking out my tongue to add extra *oomph* to my anger, I powered on, refusing to let my rant be derailed. "As I was saying, it's your fault and my *mother's* that we are under the one and only Full Cold Moon of the year, freezing our asses off. And *your* fault that we had to cut down – by hand, without Magic or the use of a chainsaw – a fifty-two-foot Hawthorne tree, chop it into logs that were exactly seventy-seven inches long, and build a Sacred Pyre that would produce Magical Golden Flames."

"But I was...."

"You were just zipping your lips and listening to what I have to say for once in your very long life. That is what you were doing," I snapped. "It was also *your* fault that we had to stomp on all those little, pointy, red berries. And you are responsible for the fact that we had to wait three weeks for a thousand-year-old wooden vat of Hawthorn mead to ferment before drinking a pint of it while the Mystical Flames of the Fire of Tailtiu, the Celtic Earth Goddess, that we had just built blazed in honor of said Deity whose sovereignty reminds us of the cyclical nature of reality and the mysteries of the deep heart which transform the ordinary into bright gold."

"Yes, I know...."

"You know that you need to keep your beak battened down, or I'mma gonna put a Spell on you that Ajax won't take off?"

"Well, I never."

"Yes, you have, you did, and you will again. It's in your nature. You got a double dose of the 'fuck with Davie gene' when you were born, hatched, or spawned onto the planet we call home. So, for the love of all that's holy, will you please shut the hell and hootenannies up and let me say what needs to be said?"

Not waiting for an answer because, honestly, I didn't give a rat's patootie what Oliver F. Plumage had to say, I just kept going. At this point, my mouth had a mind of its own, and the rest of me was merely along for the ride. "It was you and Priestess Dorothea Josephine Brown, third in line to be the Head of the Brown Family Witches and the Sorceress of the Spark of Summer, aka my mother, who convinced me to come up here to the backass of *EVERYWHERE* to perform the Ancient Ritual of Revelation and Renewal in the hopes of revealing my One True Gift before the night of the beginning of my third century, or better known as my two-hundredth birthday, so that I can keep the Magic of the Magnificent and Wonderful Brown Witches flowing through my veins and find my One True Fated Love, the man made for me by the Universe."

"You could have just called the Demi-God and Dragon Guardsman, Kayne. He is, after all, the foster grandson of...."

"Tailtiu," I ground out through teeth so tightly gritted I

could hear my jaw cracking and feel my chompers being crushed into a fine powder. "Yes, I know, but...."

"Or you could've called Molly, or Ella, or Violet, or Lottie – *your cousins*. You know, I know, and your momma knows they would've happily talked to their Mates for you. Well, all except Lottie because she hasn't found hers yet, but we all know she will. After all, those Dragons are three of the Almighty and Legendary Archer Dragons. If anyone could help you with your little problem, it...."

"My LITTLE problem?" Throwing my hands in the air, I shot up to my full five-foot-five height, stomped both my feet, and shrieked like Cousin Bathsheba Brown, the Witchy Banshee of the Brown Family Coven. "Did you really just say my LITTLE problem? What...."

"Yes, I did, because had you...."

"Had I what? What? Huh, Ollie, had I what?" Hands dropping from over my head like a meteor launched by the Celtic God of the Sky, Taranis, I shook my index finger at the very pointed beak of the little birdbrain's pouty pecker and shrieked, "Had I looked for my Mate in all the wrong places? Check!" Adding my other index finger to the party, I got even louder. "Or prayed to the Great Goddess, the Universe, the Morrígan, the Dagna, the Mother of All Witches, Destiny, Fate, and The Powers That Be to reveal my One True Gift before the expiration date tattooed on my ass comes to fruition?"

Throwing my arms open wide and letting my head fall back, I roared so loudly that my less-than-melodic voice echoed off every mountaintop. "DOUBLE CHECK!"

"But sometimes...."

"Sometimes, everyone needs a little help?" I mocked what had been said to me no less than every day since I was old enough to whip up stinky slugs and Magick them into the urinals in the boys' bathroom at Miss Oglethorpe's Academy for Wishful Witches and Warlocks. "TRIPLE CHECK!"

"Or maybe forget about the boy who gave me my first kiss behind the old, old tree?" I sassed. "Well, no check there, but I can pretend, and you can let me or incur the full force of my wrath."

Dropping my chin and arms in unison, I recounted every Spell, Incantation, Charm, Hocus Pocus, Mumbo Jumbo, Abracadabra, and Nearly Naked dance known to Witch kind ending with, "So, for you to say...." Then, making exaggerated air quotes that the 747 flying overhead at forty-thousand feet could have seen without opera glasses, I growled, "...my LITTLE problem or in any way imply that I have not done everything in my considerable Power to find not only my One True Gift but also my One True Fated Mate, then all I have to say to you is...."

"WATCH OUT BELOW!"

A roar that shook not only every leaf on every tree atop every peak in the Black Cuillin Mountains but also made my tummy do a flip-flop, my heart give a pitter-pat and my.... my.... lovely lady flower....

(Yes, I said it. No, I will not take it back. That is what I've called it for my whole life. Sure, I curse like a sailor. Absolutely, I can drink anyone and everyone under the table. I can belch the alphabet and also spit for distance. But – and this is important – I have a shit-ton of respect for my body and all its special parts and therefore choose to call that very special place of mine - my lovely lady flower. So, in your story, you can call your body parts whatever you want to. *Capisce?* Cool.)

As I was saying....

The low, rumbling baritone from overhead was unlike

anything I'd ever heard. For the first time in my long life, I knew what I had to do, why I'd been born, and most of all, how I had survived having a Familiar like Ollie for almost two-hundred years.

Head falling back, eyes looking upward, a smile had just crossed my *Perfect Peach* glossed lips when out of the clouds fell a.... a.... a.... Well, it looked like a fireball... That had wings... With flames as bright and magnificent as the sun... And so many bolts of lightning were shooting out from somewhere on its body that I wondered if a tsunami was on the way.

Faster and faster, it fell. Louder and louder, it bellowed. Bigger and bigger it became, the closer to my head it got.

And here's the most important part, Magic as Powerful as my own and that of the Brown Family Witches filled the air as said falling fireball tried with all its might to Shift from one form to another. I could see it – I mean, I could see *him* – as clear as the tip of my perfectly pert little nose on my cute-if-I-do-say-so-myself face. Sure, he was flashing from fireball to Dragon to man and back again at increasing speeds, but I could see him, and what I saw was damned fine.

His hair was the color of a sandy beach with salt and pepper streaks. His eyes were the perfect blend of gray and blue, and he had a beard I wanted to feel against my cheek. He was hot with a capital *that-man-was-made-for-me*.

Stunned, shocked, and unable to move, the little Witch in my head once again screamed, *"Move your beautiful and bodacious badonkadonk, Davina Elizabeth Brown! You're about to be...."*

But that was as far as she got.

Ignoring whatever my conscience or alter ego or proof of insanity was trying to convey, I held out my arms, ready to catch the hunka-hunka-burning love I was sure had been sent from the Heavens above just for and only me. Sure, I could've been smooshed, but I'm a Brown Witch, and we've got Dr. Bombay to put us back together. I wasn't scared.

Then, just like that, my dreams were shattered as a hole roughly the size of a mammoth's ass opened up right over the tip of the tallest Golden Flame of the Sacred Pyre Ollie and I had built. Whooshes of Wizardry blew the curly tendrils of dark hair that had fallen out of my messy bun in every direction. My eyes watered. My skin tingled. But still, I stood firm.

I didn't so much as blink as the mixed-up mishmash of manly goodness dropping to Earth flashed from fireball to Dragon to man and back again like a disco ball at Studio 54. The bolts of lightning got longer and stronger. The fireball got hotter. The ground beneath my feet quivered and quaked. It was the coolest thing I'd ever experienced. Hell, I was already getting my story straight to share with the grandkids I knew we would have in a century or two.

So, just as I was about to whip up the most extraordinary, spectacular, and super-duper Spell ever to be chanted by a Brown Family Witch in the history of the world, you might just know that three things happened to change the course of history and the well-crafted tale unraveling in my mind.

The big black hole floating over the top of the Sacred Pyre and my messy bun swallowed up the man – the Dragon – the yummy goodness I was almost totally sure was my One True Fated Mate like a pregnant Brown Family Witch eating cookies.

And....

Ollie the Asshole hit me in the gut like the entire defensive line of the 1996 World Champion Dallas Cowboys and knocked me on my ass so hard I could feel bruises forming on both cheeks of my well-rounded booty and then some.

And....

Tailtiu, the Great One of the Planet, the Celtic Earth Goddess of Rebirth, Vigor, Strength, and Endurance, flew out of the Golden Flames of the Sacred Pyre, landed not three feet from where my head hovered above the ground, and tsked, "Oh, Davina, my love. What have you gotten yourself into this time?"

Yes, I will say it again – all the planning in the world can't beat dumb luck.

As you can imagine, before I could come up with a witty retort, the Goddess I'd loved above most others gave a hearty chuckle, raised her hand, snapped her fingers, winked, and cheered me on with a sassy little, "Hang on, Sweetie. It's gonna be a bumpy ride."

Talk about things not going as planned....

Welcome to my world.

READ THE WHOLE STORY HERE!

"Dammit, Grace, pick up the phone," she growled through gritted teeth at the third voicemail she'd had to listen to in the last five minutes.

"Everything okay, Kyndel?' Barney, the *nice* guy in her office, asked.

"Yeah, everything's fine. Just trying to find Grace."

"Oh! Anything I can help with?"

Kyndel thought about telling him her troubles, but Barney had been spending an inordinate amount of time in her office lately. At first, she'd thought he was just being nice, but then he joined her hiking group, and just yesterday he showed up with her favorite no whip, nonfat, iced white chocolate mocha from the *frou frou* coffee shop on the corner. It had been then Kyndel realized she was Barney's newest crush. It had been a long time between boyfriends and Barney was nice, but...um...*no*. As flattered as she was, there was no way she was having an office romance.

'Don't shit where you eat' was one of the pieces of sage advice Granny had given her just after graduation. Not that it ever truly made sense to Kyndel, but she got the gist of it... keep your personal life *out* of the office.

She saw the puppy dog look on Barney's face and hated to crush his spirit, but Kyndel decided a brisk walk home would be better than leading the poor fellow on, in *any* way.

"No, but thank you so much." Then, to make sure he got the hint and skedaddled, she added, "Have a nice a weekend," before turning her chair and dialing Grace's office for the third time.

Voicemail *again*. Time to pack up and get the heck outta dodge before someone found something else for her to do. Bag on shoulder, scowl on face, and more than a little disgusted, Kyndel headed out of the office.

*Never loan Grace the car... Never loan Grace the car...*was the mantra playing on a loop in Kyndel's mind. She was madder than a wet hen and getting hotter by the minute. It was *no fun* to walk home after ten hours of work. *No fun* to be abandoned and forgotten by the best friend she'd loaned her car to. *No fun* to make the five-block journey past the park...in the dark.

At twenty-six, she rarely admitted her fear of the dark and held her aunts responsible for the phobia. Had they not made her watch 'The Brain Eaters' when she was only six years old, Kyndel was positive everything would've been just fine. It wasn't that she believed aliens would set loose a horde of parasites to eat every human brain on the planet; she had a *little* more sense than that. It was the feeling of being watched...like someone was hiding in the shadows, just waiting for an opportunity to scare the living daylights out of her. At the mere thought of her 'phantom stalker', the hair stood up at the nape of her neck and she walked a bit faster.

A sudden *thud,* and what sounded like footsteps pounding on the hard ground, had her stopping in her tracks. "What the...?" She gasped, opening her eyes wide, hoping it would help her see through the shadows.

Several tense seconds later—that felt like damn near forever—and Kyndel moved again. This time, her eyes slid side-to-side like the stupid black and white cat clock her granny used to have in the kitchen.

The farther she got from where she'd heard the 'thump', the easier it was to convince herself it had just been kids sneaking into the park after hours. Manlove Park was a well-known make out spot for teenagers. There might've even been a time after moving to the city when Kyndel herself had been convinced to take a walk on the wild side, but that was a story for another day.

Shoot, now I wouldn't know the wild side if I tripped and fell in it.

It had been almost a year since she'd dated the muscle-headed jock from the gym. Three long, tortuous dates and all because he had an incredible body. Of course, dating the douche bag had come at a price. She'd spent the entire time listening to him drone on about his body parts...*and not the good ones*...and *only* when he wasn't checking out every other woman in the joint.

It wasn't that he'd hurt her feelings. Kyndel knew who she was and had never been under the misconception she would be Miss America. She had a few extra pounds and her curves had curves, but she was cute and had a brain, something not everyone could claim. What had pissed her off the most about dating Vinnie was, she'd wasted three whole evenings of her life that she could never get back. The one compliment the jerk had given her had been about her skin; he thought it was beautiful. Her granny always called her complexion peaches and cream and said her freckles added character.

Yeah, cause I need more of that.

She sighed as she thought about how much of her youth she'd wasted hating those tiny brown spots, until the day she realized they weren't going anywhere. It was time to buck up and learn to love them, or stop looking in the mirror. From that day forward, she stopped using makeup to cover them and embraced her 'freckled-self'. She also learned to accept her curves. *If ya don't like em, don't look at em* was her motto. For the most part, she ate right and worked out at least three times a week. But dammit if she didn't love her Ben and Jerry's Cherry Garcia and someone would lose a hand if they tried to take it from her.

A loud *'thud'* echoed between the buildings. Kyndel stumbled to a stop. She looked and listened. The longer she thought about what she'd heard, the easier it was for her to convince herself someone had yelled for help. So, for the second time in about as many minutes, she searched the inky shadows for signs of life. Her anxiety level quadrupled the longer she stood still. She wanted to scream when only the sound of leaves rustling across the sidewalk and the occasional car passing by reached her ears.

Disgusted, she grumbled aloud, "You've gone bonkers, Kyn." The sound of her own voice somehow calmed her rankled nerves and she added, "Get to stepping, girlie."

The clicking of her heels bounced off the brick wall of the library as she hurried past. Resuming her original mantra, she added *Must kill Grace* at the end for good measure.

"I swear when I get my hands on..."

Her words were cut short as the unmistakable sound of a man groaning came from the shadows.

A chill skittered down her spine.

Goose bumps covered her arms.

She counted to three, unable to move...simply listening...praying it was only her imagination. One deep breath later, she slid her right foot forward, prepared to make a beeline for home at a high rate of speed.

The groan came again. Closer than before. More desperate...almost pleading.

The need to help the injured grew within her. Turning towards the darkness, Kyndel searched for the source of the noise.

Shaking so much her teeth chattered, she looked for any sign of the man she *knew* needed her help.

"It's time to make a decision, Kyndel. Fight or flight. What's it gonna be? God knows standing like a bump on a log isn't solving a *damn* thing."

Flight won. She turned, almost running, her satchel clutched tightly to her side like a lifeline.

"Keep your head up and eyes front. Home's only a few blocks away," she reassured herself, with the promise of snatching her best friend bald for the stupid mess she was in.

Feeling guilty and worried for Grace, her heart at war with her brain, Kyndel thought aloud, "Hope everything's okay..."

Grace had always been a little scatter-brained, but she'd never just *forgotten* Kyndel before. It bothered her that there'd been no answer at Grace's office or on her cellphone when Kyndel had tried to track her down before leaving the office. She'd even taken a chance and tried her own home because Grace had a key, but only got voicemail there, too. It was a war between anger and worry that accompanied most of her thoughts about her friend lately.

The running joke was that Grace spent most of her time hooking up with eligible bachelors she met at work. The good Lord *knew* her bestie was gorgeous; five foot nine, long raven hair, blue eyes, and a curvy body without an extra ounce of fat. To top it off, she was a first-year lawyer, with a promising career. Grace had it all...brains and beauty, the total package.

Giggling nervously, she gave herself a mental swat to the back of the head. She didn't want anything bad to happen to Grace, just a bump or bruise, even a hangnail would explain being left. If she really had just forgotten, Kyndel was going to be *pissed* and more than a little hurt.

The shadows seemed to be closing in. Fear pushed Kyndel until she was almost jogging in her sensible work heels. Looking over her shoulder, the toe of her shoe caught an uneven piece of concrete, and from one heartbeat to the next, she was falling forward. Arms flailing, mouth stretched wide in a wordless scream, the sidewalk racing toward her face, everything around her seemed to happen in slow motion. All she could think was *that's gonna leave a mark.*

Bracing for impact, she squeezed her eyes tight and prayed...then nothing happened. Opening one eye, then the other, Kyndel found herself hanging above the sidewalk, looking at a pair of the biggest feet she had ever seen—and they were sexy.

Sexy feet? I really am losing it. Wait! Why the hell am I above the concrete?

Warmth radiated from the perfectly muscled arm

wrapped around her midsection. Goose bumps emanated from the extra-large hand holding firmly to her blouse, just a little too close to her breast.

She wiggled to change position, the cushion of her well-rounded ass finding the ridges of an incredibly hard set of abs. She trembled. Her heart raced. Just the thought of the man that could hold her upright made up for all her previous mishaps.

Within just a few seconds, Kyndel's world turned on its axis. The scenery blurred as she was effortlessly spun around and immediately found herself sitting atop the body of her rescuer, looking at faded denim covering extremely muscular thighs. Laughing aloud, she asked herself,*wonder what part I'll see next?*

The same muscled arm that had saved her face from certain demise now kept her upright. She did a one-eighty, draped her legs over his thighs, with her knees barely touching the sidewalk, and got her first look at the top half of her rescuer. All she could do was gape. He was absolutely the most handsome man she'd ever seen, with features that looked like they'd been carved by expert hands.

Even with his eyes closed, he gave off the distinctive air of authority. The dim light highlighted his high cheekbones and aristocratic nose, adding to the power she felt radiating from his every pore. His perfectly formed lips made visions of passionate kisses and hot sweaty nights dance through her brain. It didn't help that all he had on was a pair of well-worn blue jeans.

She imagined that denim riding low on his tapered hips when he stood, highlighting the incredibly sexy dimples that sat on the front of his hips. She absolutely knew without looking they were there, and that simple bit of knowledge made her temperature rise another degree, despite the cool breeze.

At the touch of her fingertips against the cool skin of his neck, an electric current arced between them. Flashes of light burst before her eyes. She blinked to clear her vision, then felt for his pulse, strong and steady against her digit. Heat rose from his skin, making her worry he might have a fever. Her eyes wandered down his well-toned body. She scoffed, unsuccessfully trying to convince herself she was only checking for further injury.

Who the hell do you think you're fooling?

She continued her perusal, taking note of his massive shoulders and a chest that could've been sculpted from granite. The light smattering of hair that glistened in the shards of light from the streetlamps emphasized his nipples, which were pebbled from the cool breeze. Her mouth watered and her pulse raced.

What the hell is it about this guy? Is he doused in pheromones? Or am I in heat?

Her eyes landed on the best set of abs she'd ever seen. Unable, or maybe it was unwilling, to stop her hand, she traced the defined lines of his eight-pack, mesmerized by the feel of his skin beneath her fingers. The electricity continued to flow between them. The sound of a horn in the distance pulled her from her musing and brought her current situation into the glaring light of reality. The sexy man that had kept her from breaking her face on the concrete was out cold, and she was paying him back by sitting on his lap and copping a feel.

She scrambled to her feet, surprised her rescuer hadn't moved an inch during her less than graceful attempt to remove her butt from his lap. But there he lay, unmoving, except for the rise and fall of his chest. The longer he remained unconscious, the more panicked she became.

Looking up and down the street and cursing Grace for the hundredth time, Kyndel wished for her car. First Aid class had taught her *never* to move an injured person unless you knew what was wrong. Not that she could pick him up and carry him, anyway. The dude was *HUGE*. At least six foot-three or four, and his muscles had muscles. She prayed he hadn't hit his head on the sidewalk. A concussion could be really bad if not treated.

"You're worried about a concussion now?" She scolded herself. "You've been drooling over the guy while his head is lying on the cold, hard sidewalk. Brilliant, Kyn, just brilliant." Reaching for her satchel, she grabbed her old sorority sweatshirt from inside, wadded it up, and knelt forward to lift his head.

Her fingers tangled in his soft, brown hair. The scattered shards of light made it look like melted chocolate flowing over her skin.

Would it shine in the sun or maybe have highlights? Some lighter brown mixed with red, even a few blond streaks woven throughout?

The silky softness of his tresses turned to something wet and sticky.

Blood!

Kyndel gulped. Panic seized the breath in her lungs as the true severity of the situation smacked her in the face. She fought to keep her calm. Now, there was absolutely no denying he needed medical attention. Reaching into her bag and cursing herself for not thinking of it sooner, she dug around for her cellphone.

Coming up empty-handed, she instantly remembered plugging it into her car charger the night before, not giving it the slightest thought until that moment. Cursing and threatening death to anyone in the immediate vicinity, she sat back on her heels and thought.

All I know to do is run down the street for help.

Looking at the fallen man, then in the direction of the Mini Mart, she reasoned he'd probably be okay. She'd be gone five minutes...*tops*. Run in, use the phone, run back. It all seemed very logical, but fear something would happen to him in her absence kept her in place.

This guy was important to her. That alone had all her red flags flying and bells and whistles screaming in her brain. She tried to push her feelings aside and look at the situation with logic, but that was like holding back a freight train with her pinky finger...*not gonna happen*. Besides, her granny would most definitely haunt her and probably kick her butt if she turned her back on someone who needed help.

"No one's gonna mess with this behemoth, even if he *is* unconscious," she reassured herself. "He probably doesn't have a wallet to steal anyway."

Should she dig in his pockets to try to find one? Some kind of ID?

Nah.

She wasn't keen on trying to explain her hand in his pants if he woke up. Her cheeks warmed at the thought of touching him again.

"What are you doing out at night in just a pair of jeans and bare feet, anyway?" she asked the unconscious man. "Guess it doesn't matter. You need help, whether you're dressed properly or not."

Hooking her satchel over her shoulder, Kyndel stood and took one last look at her 'patient'. Before she had barely moved an inch, a huge, warm hand latched onto her bare ankle.

"What the hell?" she screamed, trying to pull her leg free while looking down to see what new fresh hell had befallen her.

GET THE WHOLE STORY HERE! FOR FREE!

ABOUT JULIA

Find all my stories at JuliaMillsAuthor.com!

Hey Y'all! I'm Julia Mills the New York Times and USA Today Bestselling Author of the Dragon Guard Series. I, without a doubt, admit to being a sarcastic, southern woman who would rather spend all day laughing than a minute crying. Living with my two most amazing daughters and a menagerie of animals keeps me busy, but I love telling a good story. Now, that I've decided to write the stories running through my brain, life is just a blast!

My beliefs are simple. A good book, along with shoes, makeup, and purses, will never let a girl down, and no hero ever written will compare to my real-life hero, my dad! I'm a sucker for a happy ending, and alpha men make me swoon.

I'm still working on my story, but I promise it will contain as much love and laughter as I can pack into it! Now, go out there and create your own story!!! Dare to Dream! Have the Strength to Try EVERYTHING! Never Look Back!

Take care and Read lots!

I ABSOLUTELY adore stalkers so look me up on Facebook,
sign up for my newsletter at JuliaMillsAuthor.com, and
follow me on BookBub!
Send me a message!
XOXO Julia

ALSO BY JULIA

Find Them All RIGHT HERE!

Although this epic journey travels through many Clans, many lands, and many couples, one thing remains constant -
Fate Will Not Be Denied!
Each book is written as a standalone story, but just like M&M's, Lay's Potato Chips, and my momma's queso, they're better when binged.

Dragon Guard Order
1.Her Dragon to Slay
2.Her Dragon's Fire
3.Haunted by Her Dragon
4.For the Love of Her Dragon
5.Saved by Her Dragon
Her Love, Her Dragon, A Dragon Guard Prequel
6.Only for Her Dragon
7.Fighting for Her Dragon
8.Her Dragon's Heart
9.Her Dragon's Soul

10. The Fate of Her Dragon
11. Her Dragon's No Angel
12. Her Dragon, His Demon
13, Resurrecting Her Dragon
14. The Scars of Her Dragon
15. Her Mad Dragon
16. Tears for Her Dragon
17, Guarding Her Dragon
18. Sassing Her Dragon
19. Kiss of Her Dragon
20. Claws, Class, and a Whole Lotta Sass
21. Dragon with the Girl Tattoo
22. Dragon Down
23. Twinkle, Twinkle, Sassy Little Star
24. Dragon Got Your Tongue
25. Fury
26, Dragon in the Mist
27. Dragon Got Run Over by A Reindeer
28. Tangled in Tinsel
29. Cupcake Kisses & Dragon Dreams
30. Her Dragon's Treasure
31. Aww Snap, Dragon
32. Imagine Dragon
33. Save a Horse, Ride a Dragon
34. Burn Dragon Burn
35. She Thinks My Dragon's Sexy
36. Dreamin' of a White Dragon
37. Dragon Her Home
38. Stone Cold Protector
39. Dragon's Lore
40. King Outta Water
41. Dragon, It's Cold Outside
42. Dragon, Be Mine

Dragon Guard Collections
Dragon Guard Series: Volume 1
Dragon Guard Series: Volume 2
Dragon Guard Series: Volume 3
Dragon Guard: The Thunder Rolls
Dragon Guard: Enforcers Arise
Christmas Magic: Dragon Guard Holidays Volume 1

Dragon Intelligence Agency
Dragon Falling
Dragon Dreaming

Dragon Guard Berserkers
Banning
Asher
Raynor
Dragon Guard Berserkers, Volume 1

~

Ladies of the Sky
Sadie's Shadow

~

Kings of the Blood
Viktor
Roman
Achilles
Kings of the Blood, Books 1 - 3

~

Dragons of Fate
Chestnuts Roasting Over Dragon Fire
Unwrapping Her Dragon
She Needs A Little Dragon
Falling Off Her Dragon
The Dragon of Valentine's Past
Dragons of Fate Collection, Books 1 - 4

~

Dragon of Destiny
Dragon Him Out To Sea

~

Dragon Guard Holiday Love Stories
It's The Great Dragon, Molly Brown
A Little Elfin' Around

Heart On For Dragon
Dragons Fall Hard
Dragon Guard Holiday Love Stories, Books 1 -3

Not Quite Holiday Love Stories
Kissing Cupid
Kissing Claws

Maidens of Mayhem
That Hound Don't Hunt
That Pig Gonna Fly
That Mule's Got A Kick
That Rex Gotta Roar
That Shark is Red Hot
That Dino's Hanging Ten
That Dragon Gonna Blow

Not Quite Love Stories
Vidalia
Phoebe
Zoey
Jax
Heidi
Lola
Sammie Jo
Harmony
Daphne

Magic & Mayhem Collections
The Not Quite Collection Volume 1
The Not Quite Collection Volume 2
Maidens of Mayhem Collection Volume 3
Maidens of Mayhem Collection Volume 4

Southern Fried Sass
Later Gator
Nosey Rosie
Lazy Daisy
Jamie's Got A Wand
Southern Fried Sass: Volume 1

Up Shift Creek
Tree Frog and Her Honey Badger
Doc and Her Dragon
Dusty and Her Dino

Daughters of Poseidon
Out of the Ashes
Scorched Embers

Lords of Hell

Hades Halo

❧

A Vampire's Thirst: Alaric

❧

Condemned: A Vampire Blood Courtesan Romance
Caught: A Vampire Blood Courtesan Romance

❧

Marrok: Hunger For His Mate

❧

Coloring Books
Bitch Please! I Color Dragons
Witch Please! I Color Dragons
Dragons of Legend Coloring Book

❧

Planners
The Dragon Never Sleeps
No Rest for The Dragon

❧

Reading Journals
On the Wings of Words

Dragon Guard
Holiday Love stories

Julia Mills
SASSY
10 Years & Still Flying High
WWW.JULIAMILLSAUTHOR.COM